A. GENTRY MADSEN

The Muffin Man

A Cautionary Tale

First edition

This book was professionally typeset on Reedsy.
Find out more at reedsy.com

This book is dedicated to my wonderful wife Candice, and my three boys: Aiden, Elliot, and Lincoln.

For psychopaths, it [corporate success] is a game and they don't mind if they violate morals. It is about getting where they want in the company and having dominance over others...Psychopathic behavior in the general population is about one in a 100. What's a little disturbing in this study is that not only are 21 percent of corporate executives psychopathic, but so is the same percentage of prison inmates.

GENE MARKS, THE WASHINGTON POST

Contents

Also by A. Gentry Madsen

Inspiration

Many chapters, scenes, characters and critical moments in this novella have received inspiration from music. Below is a list of those songs that inspired me:

1. All Those Yesterdays- Pearl Jam
2. Wagon Wheel- Old Crow Medicine Show
3. Under the Bridge- Red Hot Chili Peppers
4. Lost In Space- Aimee Mann
5. San Andreas Fault- Natalie Merchant
6. Strong Enough- Sheryl Crow
7. Colder Weather- Zac Brown Band
8. Growin' Up- Macklemore and Ryan Lewis
9. Red Hands (big guitar version)- Walking Off The Earth*
10. Otherside (remix)- Macklemore & Ryan Lewis
11. Sympathy for the Devil- Rolling Stones*
12. Glorified G- Pearl Jam
13. I Got Friends in Low Places- Garth Brooks
14. What I Am- Edie Brickell and the New Bohemians*
15. House of the Rising Sun- The Animals
16. Wonderwall- Oasis
17. Burning House- Cam
18. Crazy Love- Van Morrison
19. Mean- Taylor Swift
20. In the Waiting Line- Zero 7
21. Higher Love- Lilly Winwood*

22. Day of the Locusts- Bob Dylan
23. Past Lives- Langehorne Slim
24. No Rain - Blind Melon

If you wish to hear these songs, most can be purchased through Amazon Music. Some songs may only be heard through Youtube, signified by an asterisk (*)

1

Alarms

B *lue lights?* Blue lights rotating. Blue lights illuminating the dark, unreachable ceilings. Production halts as the workers stare, in awe and confusion, at the circling lights. Silent moments pass; idle hands and hushed machinery. As curiosity fades, they slowly start back into their work, preoccupied with deciphering the lights overhead. *What did they mean? Blue, hmmm, it was so long ago. What did the blue mean?——Ammonia.* A deafening alarm sounded, brash and unavoidable, sending the workers into an chaotic frenzy, followed by an indescribable but nauseating smell which quickly saturated the facility. The alarm nearly drowned out the screams of the descending supervisor. A gangly man, in his mid-thirties, with styled brown and grey hair and a patchy, overgrown beard covered in a net, awkwardly stumbled down the stairs as he rushed to the production floor. His thin, muscle-less arms flailed in a starchy, white oversized smock. After catching his glasses before they slipped from off his nose, he pointed over his head to the furthest corner of the facility, shouting what must have been directions. He fought to appear calm, for the good of the staff, while he shook with fear inside. The workers charged for the exits, covering their mouths, their eyes struck with panic. People tripped, stepping over each other, running from the invisible killer at their heels. They funneled frantically through a single door into the empty leaf-covered, windswept parking lot. Fear had them aggressively pushing and shoving their co-workers and friends, fighting to feel the sting of the frozen, clean Minnesota air. The lanky supervisor stood at the door, touching the tops of heads, keeping count. *21...31....33...Jesus, how many were there today?....35.* He kept counting, almost gagging from the smell trapped in the back of his throat, stopping briefly to pick prone workers off the floor. As the people outside began to outnumber the people inside, a slight relief washed over him. *Not many left.* The gas was now much more than just an irritating smell. It hung from his uvula and repelled down, spelunking in the caverns of his lungs; it stung fiercely like angry hornets.

"Fifty-six, fifty-seven, fifty-eight." The young man started counting aloud. The distant sirens began to grind against the alarms from inside. Pausing the line for a moment, "Find your partners, then head to the sign by the trees."

From inside he couldn't see the trucks, but he caught the lights as they peeked from behind the amassing crowd. The sirens were as loud as the alarms, but completely different in sound. It was overwhelming, all his senses were overloaded.

"Andreas!!! Andreas!!!" An older Hispanic lady rushed back toward the door as Andrew counted the last to leave. "Martina!! Martina!! no esta aqui!!! no esta aqui!!" She began grabbing at his smock, worriedly shaking his arms.

"Are you sure?" He quickly asked, but to no response. "Se-se-segura...Esta Segura?" Struggling to translate.

"Si, si, si. Ve ahora!!! Ve ahora!!!" She yelled with tears streaming down her face. Before she was able to finish Andrew turned to rush back in as the door closed.

Firefighters quickly dismounted, while police escorted the crowd to the predetermined and designated safe zone.

"Amoniaco!" The crowd shouted in warning.

"What?" A firefighter said loudly, pulling his heavy jacket on.

"Ammonia!" One of the few primarily English speaking workers explained.

"Is this everyone?" They asked, preparing for entry, situating their breathing apparatus.

"No, we're missing Martina. The supervisor went back in to find her." The firefighters made quick passage through the crowd.

"Martina!!! Martina!!!" Andrew probed the empty concourse, his chest burning more and more with each word. *Where was she working today? Ovens? No. Cutting room? No. Packaging? Was it packaging? Yes, it was packaging...right by the fifty-foot high cooling room. Jesus!* He changed direction, now sprinting to the packaging area. His nose was bleeding, not a drip or dried crunchy blood, but a stream of blood that rained down the front of his white smock.

"Martina!!!" He scanned the area; eyes panning quickly across the production floor and under the conveyors. *A faint cough, somewhere around here.* He listened closer while scrambling around the giant refridgeration unit.

"Martina!!! Martina!!!" His own voice, between coughs, ricocheted off the expansive ceilings and bare walls of the facility; battling, and winning against the alarm. *Found her.*

"Martina. Esta Bien?" He coughed between syllables. She was too weak to respond. Motionless other than her quivering

3

lips and the jump of her chest as she coughed up blood. Eyes closed, she was slumped at the conveyor as it first exited the cooling tower. Donuts piled around her body as a package sat across the still running machine, haphazardly tossing the products to either side.

Andrew bent down, his own blood now mixing with hers, and put his arms under her body. He attempted to cradle her but began to feel weak himself. He garnered his remaining strength, wrenching his shoulders back, but could not move her. The dedicated steward tried again spewing blood as he strained, it seemed futile. Weakened and dizzied himself, he collapsed to his knees, tried to catch his breath then toppled next to her. *I can't. I can't. I don't have the energy, I'm soo weak. I'm sorry Martina.* He placed a comforting hand on her chest, he couldn't rescue her, he was defeated and he knew it. *I tried.*

A lone house-fly materialized from the rafters and buzzed down, spiraling around his head with emetic speed, unplagued by the insidious gas, finally perching upon his shoulder. There it sat for uninterrupted moments, as they exchanged eternal glances. His brain struggled, labored to maintain, thoughts became sporadic, non-sequential. *Donuts, I'm going to die surrounded by donuts, fuck.* Staring at the donuts, they blurred as his field of vision narrowed, encircled by darkness. A shadowy noir figure, likened to a children's dark charcoal scribble, emerged floating, till it stood inhumanly tall before him. He looked up, squinting, his all-pupil eyes fluttering, discombobulated. He drifted circuitously through states of consciousness. It stretched to unimaginable angles then abruptly shrunk, roughly taking the shape of an older lady in all black, and curled down next to him. It whispered, 'Don't you think you ought to lay your head down,' then smashed into

millions of minuscule particles.
[Pearl Jam- All Those Yesterdays]

2

Progress Report

"Do you see her yet?" A woman in formal business attire covered in a white smock, adorned with a 'visitor' name-badge paced back and forth in the main entry.

"No, she should be here soon though." A young but exhausted lady responded from behind the desk. "Could I have you sign this log before she gets here?"

"Sure." As she scribbled 'Clara Foster- OSHA' in the visitor log book, followed by the badge number she was assigned. "How is everyone doing? Are you the only one here today?"

"Most everyone is fine. Troy is here, he's the other supervisor that was here last night. He's down the hall on the left if you want to talk to him first." The receptionist responded in a reserved and sullen tone. Troy was in his very early twenties, he had been a temp worker who was promoted to supervisor a few years prior.

"No, thank you. I'll wait." She settled into the uncomfortably modern chair facing away from the entry. The early morning sun flooded the entry from the bay windows. Not a cloud in the sky, not completely untypical for an October morning.

It was before rush hour and cars barely dotted the road that passed outside. The parking lot was empty, minus four cars. The receptionist thumbed through the carousel of single serve coffees, finally settling on the Breakfast Blend. Pressing the start button, she stared down at the machine, waiting for it to finish.

"Would you like one? She always makes sure we have a great assortment...makes mornings easier." The aroma was welcoming and reviving.

"No, I'm fine." Clara said, looking up while paging through her reports. A yawn escaped, and her eyes watered. 'This could be a long day', she thought. "Actually, sure."

The receptionist brewed a cup for her. She removed a few of the baking industry and business magazines from the table next to Clara and set the cup down gently on a coaster, then resumed her previous business.

"Won't be much longer I'm sure." She said from behind the desk, as Clara sipped her coffee, giving her a nod of approval and appreciation.

The lights at the nearest intersection changed, changed, changed, and changed again. Buses began to pick up riders, and the roads became more congested. The office phone started ringing, the receptionist answered with a warm greeting, said a few unintelligible words, thanked them and hung up. The phone rang again, and again and again. Soon, her greetings were shorter and she was asking them to hold. More calls, she was now writing down numbers to call back because she was unable to place anymore on hold. Her voice was slowly changing from warm to hurried, to worried and finally to frantic.

"I see her car. She's here." The receptionist covered the

mouthpiece of the phone as she leaned over the desk pointing to an SUV out to the window. A diminutive woman nearing sixty or sixty-five struggled to place a foot on the ground as the Lexus had a very high clearance. It was new, not this year or last, but this week. It still had the paper plates that came from the dealership, and the tires shined like they had never seen a road or a Minnesota pothole. She couldn't have been much more than five feet tall, and had jet black hair, obviously dyed. Botox treatments were unable to silence the stories hidden within the lines of her brow. Her heels looked severely out of place, and her attire, similar to Clara's, was that of someone who worked in the corporate world not a bakery.

"What's this about?" She asked in a perturbed voice as she entered through the glass doors, not getting a response. "Hey! Why is it zero?" She yelled, pointing at the 'injury-free' work days counter. "Someone stub a toe again?" She mumbled under her breath, laughing to herself.

"Patty, this is Clara." Clara stood up, tugging on her skirt and extending a hand. "She's with OSHA." Patty shook her hand then sternly gazed back at the receptionist, as if saying 'why didn't you tell me first, bitch'.

"Oh, good morning Clara. We can talk in my office. Just give me a minute." Patty spoke comfortably and business-like but with curious sincerity.

"Certainly." Clara said a little irritated, and sat back down.

Patty headed down the hall, her heels clicking against the polished concrete. She barely poked her head in the office, when Troy turned and stood up from the chair facing the desk. His shoulders slouched, eyes swollen and weary pressing to stay attentive after sixteen hours. He looked like a strung out frat boy.

"What the fuck Troy! What is OSHA doing here?" An angry whisper with terrible intent.

"Las—"

"And why isn't there anyone here?" She stopped him short.

"Last night there was an Ammonia leak. Everyone had to exit the building."

"So, why aren't they here today?!" Patty slammed her purse down on her desk and stood in front of Troy as he sat back down, leveraging her power. "No staff, no production, no production, no *MONEY*!"

"Ther—"

"Get them here now." She demanded, squinting and motioning toward the door. Troy tried to analyze her request and the improbability of it happening, and cringed at the thought of it.

"It's not that simple, Patty." A voice snuck in from the other side of the door. "I'm sorry, but this requires your attention *now*." Clara responded to her demand of Troy. Troy pushed his chair back, stood up and exited the room, feet dragging. "I will need to speak to you as well Troy."

While Clara faced Troy as he left the room, Patty looked him directly in the eyes and pointed her right index finger into her left palm, mouthing 'Get them here NOW!'. Troy broke the contact short and looked toward the floor. With no college in his past or seemingly in his future, the opportunity to be a supervisor, which Patty presented him with, seemed to be a great career path. He didn't it know at the time, but Patty typically promoted or hired people she felt she could control or manipulate or blackmail. Most her supervisory staff had something she could hold over them, or a button she could push on demand that would alter their behavior. Troy was now too involved and invested to just leave; she had him.

"Did you need a coffee or a pistachio muffin? They are our specialty, I could have Stacy—-." Patty attempted to placate her visitor, pulling the chair out.

"No, I'm fine. Sit. Please. Last night there was an ammonia leak here."

"Yes, I am aware of that." The plant manager said from her Italian leather high-backed executive chair. Adjusting the height so that she was a few inches higher than Clara. "We will go over procedure and training, we wouldn't want anyone to get hurt. Ammonia is necessary, but dangerous. It is unfortunate."

"It is Patty. Two of your employees are in the hospital." Clara spoke, not buying into Patty's charade. Patty looked momentarily stunned.

"Oh?"

"One is in critical condition, the other serious. I am here to find out how and why it happened. And, if proper procedure was followed…if it was preventable."

"Anything you need, anyone you need to talk to. Just let me know, we'll help however we can."

"Is the area safe to enter yet?"

"Umm. Troy!" Patty deferred to the youngest supervisor, loud enough to carry down the hallway, but not loud enough to cause concern.

"Yes." He said, standing in the doorway. Not having moved fast enough to fully exit earshot.

"Has the leak been found? Is the area safe?"

"Well, the leak has not been found, but we did close the emergency shut off valve and placed the ventilation on max, which should clear the production floor in about an hour or so."

"Oh, Thank you Troy." *Thank you? Thank you? Shes never said that before, what a joke.* "Please take Clara to the production area once it's safe, I appreciate your help. And Troy, I'm so glad you're safe." *Seriously, what a joke.* Troy was pissed and exhausted, hardly enough strength to muscle a response, but smart enough to play along.

"Thank you Patty." He managed a smile, he'd had months of experience training the muscles of his face to imitate genuine responses when prodded by his boss.

Patty and Clara continued with the conversation. Troy was sure Patty gave her the same treatment she gave anyone important that could aid or impede her own success. Power was everything to Patty; it kept her safe. When it was challenged she was capable of playing into it, numbing the opposition with an unrivaled but veiled kindness until she was able to catch them off guard and reverse the roles. Power was self-preservation.

Troy could hear the latch off the door. If Clara wasn't prepared and strong, she'd soon be the one apologizing and thanking Patty. Walking back toward the entry, he could hear a familiar voice.

"They're where?" A round, bulky man with stark white hair tugged haphazardly across the growing bald spot atop his head said while tucking his monogrammed blue uniform shirt into his matching pants. A loveable, loquacious fellow, Art was a cab driver in his past life, until his growing girth hindered his ability to fit comfortably behind the wheel. His hospitality and people-skills followed him to the bakery.

"The hospital...St. Anthonys." Stacy, the receptionist, calmly answered.

"Art."

"Troy, you doing alright? How's Andrew, you talk to him?"

Adjusting his waistline as it fought against his enormous belly.

"I'm alright Art. Haven't talked to him, just family now. I called them last night, but you know how that situation is now."

"Not so good then, huh. What about Martina?"

"Well, I can't get ahold of any of the family she listed on her emergency contact form. They're all disconnected or Mexican phone numbers, no one close. The doctors told us it's not good. Critical condition. Sounds like she had the longest and harshest exposure.—-Poor lady."

"Jesus. I'll stop by the hospital after work. She was the nicest lady."

"OSHA is here."

"Really? I saw Patty's new car, at least I'm guessing it's hers. Only one here that could afford it."

"Yeah, she's here, enjoy the show. She's doing the 'I'm sorry, remorseful' routine with the OSHA lady. She even thanked me." Troy said with a soft chuckle. For as much as he disapproved of her methods, he secretly applauded their effectiveness. Blessed with a natural gift for office politics, this gift told him it was wise not to disclose his thoughts to his colleagues.

"God, it's disgusting. Not many cars out there, I'm assuming production is on hold?" The old man shook his head, repulsed but not shocked.

"Yeah, Patty loves it. We need to find the leak and get it repaired before we can start working again. It must be some-where close to the cooling tower where they—-umm—-where they found them."

3

Opportunity Costs

"Looks like it's coming from up here." Troy pulled his mask away for a moment and yelled down from a lift, showing them the pink litmus paper. "I'll try to find the exact spot."

After fixing his mask, he lit a sulfur stick and ran it around, back-and-forth down the 10-inch overhead pipes multiple times. The flame began to flicker and let off white smoke.

"Found it, move me up and forward a few more inches so I can see the other side of this pipe." The lift moved slowly, as Troy grasped the railing, his safety harness carabineers banging against them. *Shit, it's huge.* A crack a half inch wide ran across a good two feet of pipe. Directly below him was the conveyor exit where they found Martina and Andrew. Troy signaled them to bring him down.

"We can shut off the gas again. We're going to have to replace at least two feet of pipe." As he unhooked himself and stepped off the lift.

Clara began to scribble notes down on her yellow legal pad as they headed back toward the breakroom. Patty, always, in step with her adversary. Troy and Art a few paces behind, quietly speaking amongst themselves.

"Hey." Troy nudged Art with his elbow, attempting to get his attention without attracting the others. "Wasn't that?" He said like he just remembered something, looking toward the pipes.

"Yeah." Art indicated before Troy could finish his question. They both shook their heads, ending the conversation as Patty's chin aligned with her shoulder and her eyes darted in their direction. Like trained dogs they heeled.

After hanging up their masks and smocks, all but Troy settled into poorly kept cafeteria chairs around a folding table. Yesterdays lunches, coffees, and donuts still holding the spots they did before the alarms.

"Troy, could you clean this up and grab us some coffee? Thanks." Her question, more of a command to the exhausted high-school dropout working on his seventeenth straight hour of work. Without answering he began to collect the items that littered the table.

"We can have that length of pipe removed and replaced by tomorrow." Hoping that would be sufficient, she turned to her stout supervisor. "Art. I thought these checks were being covered on the 'CI' pre-op checklist. Probably would've identified the problem before the shift."

"Sure." Art acknowledged, playing his part in her little production. *It aint on there, plus if it was, we aren't gonna examine three-thousand feet of pipe fifty feet in the air before EVERY shift. Jesus.* He smiled, and nodded positively.

"Thank you." Patty said to Troy as he placed Styrofoam cups in front of them. "Cream? Sugar?" She looked to Clara.

"No thank you." She said, noticing the not-so-covert demeaning treatment. "Maybe those checks could be done monthly or quarterly. I think that might be sufficient." Trying to find a suitable middle ground.

"Either way, I think we need to pay more attention to our environment. From the CI reports, I thought it was being taken care." Troy opened a coffee creamer and began pouring it in Patty's cup, knowing what she liked. Then, quasi-intentionally spilled some of the creamer on her hand around the cup. "It's fine, it's fine!" She jumped a little, then grabbed a napkin from the dispenser and cleaner it off, leering at Troy with a smile that screamed 'I'm going to cut your fucking balls off'.

"I see you have an SQDC board." Clara said as she looked around the room. "Looks like mostly green days for Safety."

"Yes, we pride ourselves in our commitment to employee safety." Patty responded pridefully. Both Troy and Art fought hard to hold back a scoff caught in their throats. *She looks like she really believes it.* "We have won many company awards for CI and 5S."

"Do you have records of previous months from the SQDC board?" Clara turned toward Art. Her chair legs a little uneven, tilting back and forth as she shifted.

"Sure do. We have them as far back as you need. They're all in a folder on the computer." Patty looked a little concerned with Arts answer.

"Think I could take a look?"

"Yeah. I could send you them to ya in an email if that works?"

"Thank you." She pulled a business card clipped to her yellow legal pad and slid it across the table. Pattys hand darted out before Arts, and secured the card.

"Thanks, we'll get that out to you today. Was there anything else you needed to see, or are we all set?" Patty asked.

"If I could just have some time with Troy to talk about the incident. That might wrap it up then."

"Of course, you can have my office, its quiet and private."

The foursome picked up their coffee cups and disposed of them. Clara continued to look around and take notes as they headed back to the entry and office area. Patty and Art stopped at the entry, while Clara and Troy continued down the hall to the offices. With a 'humpf' Patty straightened her dress coat and began picking the white lint left behind from the production smock. She kept picking at it, getting more frustrated by the moment. As frustration mounted she reached over the reception desk and grabbed a lint roller and began removing any indication that she had been in the bakery.

"There isn't anything in those files are there?" Looking at her fat colleague while the lint brush rolled down her arms.

"Nothing about ammonia."

"Don't care what it is. Green. Change them to green." The cantankerous old curmudgeon ordered him, while handing the lint roller back to Stacy.

"But—."

"For your own sake, you'd better hope they're green." She said, jamming the business card into his fat belly. "Stacy, call the contractor and get them out here to fix that pipe. And, send some flowers to Andrew and Maranda."

"You mean Martina?" Stacy carefully corrected here.

"Yes, of course, that's what I meant. See if there are any 'BOGO' deals." Patty said trying to play off the mistake. "Let everyone know we're open tomorrow. We can't afford another day like this."

"Right away." Stacy acknowledged and picked up the phone.

Meanwhile, in the office, Clara examined the room a little more while walking through the situation from the previous night with Troy. The desk a deep, rich mahogany, not the

16

cheap all-in-one things you find at office supply stores. The chair looked possibly imported, the dark leather was beautiful, seams straight and flawless, a very slick chair. Against the wall was a beautiful glass case filled with awards; Drury Lane #1 Cost Per Unit 2003, 2004, 2005, Drury Lane #1 CI scores 2003, 2004, 2005. Behind the desk were two, seven-foot tall bookshelves filled with business books and self-improvement material, and binders; all uniform with a piece of red tape that ran up-then-down, from left-to-right in horizontal fashion so that all the binders remained in the proper place. The only thing missing from the office were personal effects. It was completely sterilized, void of personality, it could have belonged to anyone or no one.

"Mis en place. Very tidy, very neat, orderly." Clara said.

"You know a little about Continuous Improvement huh?"

"A little, looks like you guys run this place pretty well."

"We try, everyone pitches in." Troy said.

"You seem to care very much about this place and the employees, so I'll just be direct." Clara said after she felt comfortable to probe further. "Is this a safe environment to work? Is there anything I should know about?" She extended the opportunity to Troy.

"I don't believe so." Troy responded quickly, not able to summon the courage to answer truthfully. Her wrath was swift, brutal and unforgiving.

"Does Patty care about work safety?" Clara asked pointedly, immediately after Troy answered, as if this was the question she meant to ask all along.

"Oh yes, yes she does." Troys mouth spoke differently from the memories that swirled in his head; the time she refused to buy steel-tipped shoes for the employees even though it was mandated by HR, the time she gave an employee with work restrictions toilet duty just to be spiteful, the fact that she never filed on-the-job work injuries to HR unless it was completely unavoidable, the six months she made everyone work through their breaks just to hit production numbers.

"Sure?" Clara wasn't satisfied with his answer and extended the opportunity once more.

"Yes."

"Alright. So, why don't you tell me what happened last night. Then you should get out of here and get some rest, I'm sure you're exhausted." That line of questioning was going nowhere so she dropped the topic.

Troy thanked her then began to chronical the events of last night. He was responsible for the West production area, separate from Andrews East production area, with its own separate emergency exit and EAP-Emergency Action Plan. Although the leak emanated from the East area, the alarms are connected through the whole facility. In the event of such an emergency, both areas are to exit the building, then are to meet in the far parking lot to take a second head-count. They are then to communicate that to the emergency first responders, who then go into the building if anyone is missing.

"So, the lights came on before the alarms sounded?" Clara asked, after Troy described the night.

"Yes, maybe a minute." Troy said as she ran a highlighter over some over her notes.

"Could be an important minute." She softly spoke, looking up from her pad. "And, Andrew headed back in? Was that part of procedure?"

"No, but, he cares about the people and I'm sure when he found out about Martina he just reacted."

"True, but it could cost him his life."

"So, he's selfless to a fault. I mean it's not something I would have done, but, I'm not going to speak negatively about it."

"And, what about those that aren't selfless. Those that care only about themselves?" A little off topic, but she said what needed to be said. She didn't expect a response, and didn't get one either.

The two got up, shook hands and left the office. Patty and Art waiting in the lobby.

"Well, again, if there is anything else. Please just give us a call." Patty still tried her charm, Clara nodded gratefully but unaffected.

"Thank you, I will be touch when my findings are complete." Clara said as she left the lobby.

"I don't want her here again!" Patty squeezed through her gritted teeth, then forced a smile and wave as Claras car backed out. "Do you understand?" Both supervisors nodded while Stacy pounded at the keyboard. "Go home and shower Troy, you look like shit." She said while slamming the door to her office.

"Glad that's over. Christ. It's like water-boarding." A relieved Troy said quietly.

"Clara grilled ya huh? She seemed alright to me."

"I meant Patty." Troy said in a tired, faint chuckle. "So, didn't you recommend that pipe be replaced on the last CapEx request?"

"Yeah, last year. That piping is actually outdated and not up to current code."

"So, why didn't it get done?"

"Patty decided the CapEx money was better spent else-where...like her office. She said we had to look the part of a professional bakery. I think she just wanted somewhere to keep her trophies."

4

Motives

"Andrew to my office, Andrew to my office." The intercom blared Pattys voice throughout the facility, piercing through the ambient noise.

"Lucky you." Art chuckled as Andrew spun around in his chair.

"Chop, chop young buck." Lindsay said, clapping his hands. "Been nice knowin' ya." They all laughed together.

Andrew trotted down from the crows nest. His heavy boots, clanking off the steel steps. The cutting line paused, they all looked at him, thinking this could possibly be the last time they saw him. He smiled and nodded and they continued their work. The sweet smell of coffee cake, pistachio muffins and streusel made it hard to be nervous or concerned, but he was. He hadn't heard anything from Patty since he returned to work. *This could be bad.*

He passed the lobby, nothing seemed to be different, nothing caused him to be alarmed. As he approached Pattys office, he heard her on the phone and waited outside until she was finished. Her tone on the phone was calm, almost even considerate.

"Andrew. Come in, sit down. How are you? I'm so glad you're doing better." She smiled and waved him in, even pulling the chair out for him.

Now, he was alarmed. This was abnormal to say the least. *What the hell? Who ARE you?* Shocked, he couldn't even manage a syllable.

"How is your family? How is your little girl?" She continued.

"Ummm, boys. Two. Christopher and Parker." He said, emphasizing the 's' in boys. He was still cautious. And, chose not to elaborate. "They're good." He added, seeing how she waited from him to finish.

"That's good. Say, I ordered new flour, baking soda and shortening from Baxters for the Holiday Fruit Cakes. Tis' the season ya know." She laughed peculiarly, and for longer than socially acceptable. "It's supposedly pretty good. Could you see how it is for the next couple months?"

"Wel—"

"If your worried about the formulas, they've been approved by R&D and accounting. They just haven't updated the system to reflect it yet." She reassured him.

"Well, that's fine then. Is that it?" Andrew asked, still waiting for her to destroy him. A student of the Oreo sandwich corrective criticism method, Andrew half-expected her to follow with the soul-crushing, sweet cream center.

"Yes." She said, leaving him the opportunity to ask anything else.

"Alright, thanks." Andrew stood and approached the doorway.

"Oh, and if for some reason there are any defectives. I don't believe there should be. But, if for some reason there are, could you save them for me? Just set them aside." Patty still smiling, the corners of her lips shook from holding the uncomfortable position.

"Yeah, I guess so." Andrew left the office completely dumbfounded, and nervous. *Did something change over-night? A new medication? I always thought she was a little bi-polar. God, I'm an ass. Maybe she is trying.*

Outside the office, he turned his head back, checking to see if what just happened, actually happened. Astonished he shook his head, a little disappointed at himself for his limited faith in her.

On his way back to the production floor, the intercom blared once more. "Attention everyone. Attention." She cleared her throat. "I am very sorry to say that Martina has passed. There will be services held at Our Lady of Guadeloupe Church in St. Paul on Monday, November Seventh at twelve thirty pm. Please feel free to take an extra hour for lunch if you wish to attend. The address and directions are available in the lobby. Thank you." Her voice grew softer and softer with each sentence.

The production floor was somber, quiet, except for Martina's friends at the packaging line who were leaning on each other, holding tight, trying to console the other while they cried themselves. One fell to the floor in hysterics, then immediately ran to the restroom while screaming "Oh mi Jesus, Oh mi Jesus, perdonanos nuestros pecados...". Many people looked around bewildered waiting for someone to tell them what to do, or how to act. A few minutes after the final crackle of the intercom, the machines slowly started up across the facility, but other than the mulling of the machines the facility was hushed. All doing their work with silent, sullen motions; not knowing what could or should be said. *I am an ass. She is trying, you could hear it in her voice. Everyone could hear it.*

23

A week passed and all were amazed at the transformation they witnessed in Patty. Sure, there were some who still had contempt for her and others that were still not sold by her behavior. But, in the past week she had not insulted anyone, asked anything unethical of her supervisors, or objectified any of her employees. There was something to be said for that.

It was colder than normal for early November, and the wind added a sting to the chill. A few leaves still danced around the parking lot, and caught themselves under tires or windshield wipers. The color of fall was almost gone. Troy entered his sedan and slid his seat forward to make room for his travelers. The supervisors piled in, it was tight in back but the trip wasn't far. Monday had come fast. Troy started the car up, turned on the radio then straightened his hand-me-down tie in the rearview mirror.

[Wagon Wheel- Old Crow Medicine Show]

"It's still hard to believe." Troy said.

"It feels surreal. She was such a nice lady." Andrew added.

"And, to think she could still be here." Art reminded everyone. "Hard to stomach."

"What do you mean?" Andrew asked.

"No one told you?" Troy looked at Andrew in the mirror, while trying to keep an eye on the road.

"Told me what?"

"Those pipes were supposed to be replaced last year. They're not up to code." Art said.

"Are you fucking with me?" Andrew was pissed. *And to think I believed that bitch.* "I almost died from that." His neck strained, his chest tightened and his pupils jostled. *Calm down, calm.*

"Calm down all yas. We're going to be there in a second." Lindsay said. The grizzly old mans cigarette hung out the cracked window, his white dress shirt yellowed from years of smoke.

"When were you going to tell me?"

"We thought you knew. But, I guess- yeah- Phil was here. Sorry." Troy said.

"No problem, I'm not pissed at you." Andrew said as he let out a few last deep breathes, trying to clear his mind.

The cathedral poked out above the buildings and pierced the low looming clouds. A black hearse waited in front of the entrance. Over the last week, the supervisors had collected donations to provide the casket and burial plot. Since no family could be found, they tried to arrange a funeral they believed she would appreciate and approve of. The men pulled into the parking lot, and slowly exited the car. Andrew, who squeezed in the middle of the back seat, was the last to exit. He had a hand on the door and one on the frame about to pull himself out.

"You all settled?" The pragmatic, old Marlboro man stood in front of him and asked as he took a final pull from his cigarette then smothered it under his loafers. "Cause we don't need a scene." Lindsay blew out the smoke, and it immediately got whipped up into the sky.

"I'm good. I'm good." Andrew said. Lindsay moved out of his way and gave the young man a hand out. And, they all proceeded to the church.

The pews were only about a quarter filled, almost all Drury Lane employees. The aisle was lined with flowers left-over from the All Saints Day service a week earlier. The walls flickered with white candles. In the front pew were Martina's three friends and Patty. In front of them was a beautiful wreath of poinesttias, roses, and carnatios, all white surrounding a large picture of Martina; as was custom of Spanish funerals. To the side of the wreath and picture was a modest white casket, inside Martina was adorned with more flowers and her wood rosary. She looked peaceful. *Martina, I'm sorry I wasn't able to help you.*

"It's not your fault." A soft voice whispered in consolation, while laying a hand upon his shoulder.

"I-" Andrew said while turning his head. *Patty!* "I know." He said softly, trying to mimic her tone, while holding his aggression back. *It's your fault you fucking cunt.* He gently removed her hand off his shoulder.

"Sometimes things just happen that are out of your hands." She continued. "Accidents. No one is to fault. You couldn't have saved her, try not to dwell." Still speaking softly as she gave a look that was a wretched mix between a smile and a frown. *Is she playing with me? Toying with me?* She arose and walked back to the pew, standing amongst Martina's friends.

The mass continued, without interruption. It was shorter than normal Hispanic funerals due to monetary restraints, but the sentiment remained. Patty looked the part of a grieving friend and colleague; she spoke fondly of her and drove Martinas friends in the procession. She looked sad when it was prudent and cried when those around her did the same. Andrew was truly confused.

When the bakery staff returned to the facility, the break room tables were stacked with Donatellos pizza boxes, the grease soaking through to the table tops. The entire staff, now clad in their production gear, flooded into the break room. They entered; some still somber, others ready to work, but now, after seeing the pizza, most were a little confused, many felt bewildered.

"Pizza party!" Patty walked in from the office hallway. "I felt we all needed this. Martina was a great woman. You are all great people. Thank you." Her voice was excited, a complete flip-flop over a matter of an hour. "Go ahead, take what you want. There is a cooler here full of pop as well. Please….help yourselves." She said as everyone stood unmoving, still deciding what the appropriate course of action should be.

"What the hell?" Andrew whispered to Lindsay, giving him a nudge.

"Whatever. It's pizza." The stinky old man, tucked the cigarette pack in his breast pocket then hopped to a table, grabbing a plate and a couple slices.

"Can you believe this?" Andrew moved over to Frank.

"Donatellos is the best man. You had their Cubano Pizza?" Frank said as he walked off to grab a pop and a chair. Andrew couldn't believe it. *Is everyone stupid?*

"Aren't you gonna eat?" Patty slithered over to him and asked with a smile. The smile spoiled it all; it stretched from ear to ear and screamed 'I win, I always win you little pissant.' She was fucking with him.

"Oh yeah, thanks Patty. I love pizza." He said, thinking something entirely different.

5

Monetized

"Thirty-thousand dollars, gentlemen. Thirty-thousand dollars." Patty repeated, while circling behind the supervisors in the meeting room. "Ridiculous, she hit us up with a thirty-thousand dollar fine. The citation said that the situation could have been avoided. Now would anyone like to clear the air and tell me how she decided that?"

The room remained silent, every supervisor looking either down, across the table or at the clock. Anything to avoid locking eyes with the beast.

"What I expected, no worries. I will find out, I have ways." Slapping the table, then calmly sitting down at the head chair. "Moving on. Have we started looking for a replacement for Maranda?"

"Martina." A still suffering Andrew said under his breath. "And, can we stop speaking about her like she's a burnt out lightbulb? Jesus." A fire burned under his tongue. Apparently having been hospitalized emboldened him, making him less vulnerable to her mindgames.

Patty smirked and chuckled. *This brazen, little, self-absorbed prick is NOT going to challenge me in front of others.*

"She is replaceable. Everyone is replaceable if I may remind you!" She threatened him, and slammed her open palms against the table again. "See if you can find someone with the same 'qualifications' as her?"

"And what would those be?" Andrew challenged again.

"Cheap and no commitment."

"She was committed."

"I wasn't talking about her. I was talking about us. No commitment. No benefits, no privileges, and no ability to sue. Unless, of course, they'd like to head back to Mexico."

Everyones eyes wide open, mouth agape over the surreal scene unfolding before them. *She didn't just say that did she? She's losing it. Now, she's not even trying to hide it. At least before she kept some of these thoughts to herself.* The whole table started to feel nauseated, uneasy. *Could she really be this callous, unscrupulous? Are we really going to look for illegal aliens?*

"Try that temp agency. What was it called- Ace or Award? Anyway, they have hundreds of 'qualified' people waiting to work." She walked toward the door, knocking on the door frame as she headed out and laughed. The gauntlet had been laid down. The supervisors leaned back in their chairs, some looking at the ceiling, some with their head in their hands, some slowly sipping on their Diet Coke, all jolted by what just happened. They looked at each other completely aghast, waiting for someone to break the silence.

"So, are we really gonna do this?" Andrew asked rhetorically.

"We've been hiring temps from there for years." A senior supervisor retorted.

"Yeah, but we weren't consciously looking to exploit some-one's citizenship status." Troy said, backing up Andrew. "It's different now."

"I don't agree with Patty, but I don't see how its much different." One of the newer supervisor said. Some nodded, some shook their heads. The room was split. Patty still had solid control of many of the supervisors. This would be a test, a dividing point.

"Well, y'all can decide what you like. I have about three months 'till retirement. I'm not getting mixed up in this." Lindsay, the old man reeked of cheap cigarettes and wore a mustache the color of yesterdays whiskey, grumbled as he excused himself. He had a standoffish and laissez-faire way about him.

"Insubordination or compromise your integrity. Not much of a choice. You know she'll fire you if you challenge her. Remember Phil?" Frank, the silver fox, reminded everyone.

"Must have been before my time." Andrew said.

"Oh, he was. Right before you. You actually have his job. You can thank Patty for that. She ruined him. He's living with his parents. Forty years old, can't get a job. Said he sexually harassed her. She blackballed him. He's radioactive, no one will touch him." Frank leaned back in his chair, cracking his knuckles behind his head.

"So, why didn't anyone say anything?" Andrew asked.

"I've got three kids, he's got student loans, he's got his first stable job: we've all got our reasons." One of the supervisors said. "We're not proud of it. It just is what it is. My vote is we just do what she asked."

"I second that." Another supervisor said, then another, and another. The vote was in. Not unanimous, but it was obvious that no one really liked the idea of going against Patty. One by one they left the room till only Art and Andrew were left. Sitting across from each other, Andrew looking frustrated and defeated and Art looking sympathetic but attempted to console.

"Don't beat yourself up over it man." Art shared. "It's taken me years, but I've learned to just let it be. She's not going anywhere. There are fights worth fightin', and buddy this ain't one of them."

"But—ugh. You just can't- I-I just can't. She can't just get away with this." He fumbled the words, almost inconsolable and his face filled with blood. "It's not right."

"The world has enough martyrs. That's all you'll be. We'll all hope for the best, of course, but eventually you'll just be another Phil. Another casualty." Art said, trying to be helpful and supportive, but at the same time honest. Which both competed against each other in this circumstance. "Just let it go. Maybe your wife was right." He said as he collected his papers, and knocked them against the table. "Hang in their bud." He tapped Andrew's shoulder then exited the room.

Andrew, alone, left to his thoughts. There was an epic struggle raging in his head. He tried to stay calm and weigh the pros and cons of following through with her requests. His mouth watered. *This Diet Coke isn't gonna cut it.* The stress crashed like a wave against a beach, but like the ocean, there was never just one wave, it was a constant ebb and flow, crash and undertow, and he was currently treading water. Just as he was about to let out an animalistic 'arghh' of mounting frustration, Stacy came in and began cleaning up the table.

"She's a bitch." Stacy said matter-of-factly, cleaning up the table. Andrew laughed a little which calmed him down enough to breath freely.

"Thanks." He smiled, and she looked back with a look that said 'been there, don't mention it'.

He didn't have a shift today, but came in just for the meeting.

31

Which he does every time, and every time he wonders why he does it. He spent more time at work than at home, and brought all the pent-up frustration with him. Dedicating his entire young adult life to his career made many of the 'things that should have been important' merely 'things that stunted the height of his success'. Walking out to his less-than-middle-class Saturn Vue, he tried to avoid thoughts of Patty and thoughts of how he used to deal with the stress.

On the back of the late-model SUV was a stick family decal; father, mother, son, son, dog, cat. The oldest, most worn decal, the 'co-exist' decal was faded and looked like it was barely hanging on, just above the mandatory black and white license plates. He settled in, put the keys in the ignition and turned it to 'ACC'. The unit in his middle console beeped, he grabbed the black hand-set, took a deep breath and blew strong and hard. It blinked green and he started the car up, then adjusted the rear-view mirror which currently reflected the empty car seats. *Don't, don't, just don't.*

Sitting at a red light, Andrew's thoughts stirred, churning sediment to the surface; they were becoming in-ignorable. It was before noon, but there were still plenty of cars on the road, which slowed traffic, giving his thoughts even more time to creep around. *Maybe my wife was right.* Then he started thinking about their last conversation. Her words echoed in his head, 'You can't save everyone, you can't dedicate your life to work…You have a family, no number of promotions can replace that. You need to decide what's more important to you…I fell in love with YOU, NOT your job'. She still didn't understand the stress he felt from work, the situations he had to deal with, the horror of Patty. It was impossible to empathize with him. Constantly having his integrity challenged was chipping away at his inner well-being. It always came back to supporting the family, but now, his family wasn't there. *If I'm not doing this for my family, then who am I doing it for?* What started innocently enough as naïve ambition morphed into an unhealthy devotion. Since they left the house, he'd been drinking almost daily, trying to avoid the inevitable cascade of grief that loomed overhead. This, of course, was the reason for the DUI paraphernalia.

The blood slowly returned to his knuckle as he loosened his grip of the steering wheel. Andrew picked up the black unit and blew into it, allowing him to continue his drive. A familiar sight ahead, Andrew slowed the car, and pulled into the empty parking lot. Sweaty, shaky hands anticipated a future regret. Just as he unbuckled his seat belt, opened the door and stepped out, something caused him to jump back in the car. In his drivers side mirror he saw the Lexus speed into a vacant parking spot behind him. The personalized license plates read CAKEGAL. The door opened and he watched her walk into the store. *What the hell?* He leaned back in his car, debating his next move: go inside, wait till she leaves, or get the hell out of here. Andrew worked on his breathing, paying attention to the time between breathes, and feeling his chest rise and fall. Running out of methods he began reciting prayers in his head. [Under the Bridge- Red Hot Chili Peppers] *Grant me the serenity to accept the things I cannot change....*

His breathing normalized and after a few moments she returned with a non-descript brown bag. Once inside the car she cracked the perforated cap off an airplane bottle and took a few swigs, looked around, threw it out the window, finally pulling out of the parking lot. After the Lexus left his view, he felt able to breath again, looked at the store, shook his head then began the ritual of starting his car. A ragged and dirty drunk staggered across the empty lot to pick up the discarded airplane bottle, tossing back any remaining drops, his rotten tongue lewdly wiping the bottle clean, then licking the poison from his lips, wholly unembarrassed by his behavior. The drunkard tore his gaze from the bottle, to see Andrew witness this, and made a crazed growling sound then yelled something indecipherable. He approached the drivers window, dragging his unwashed fingers across the glass in an unsettling and pitiful manner. Andrew slowly backed up while the man fell to his knees and groveled with a sad patheticism. After a distance his groveling turned to vengeful anger as he threw a handful of snow and dirt at the Saturn, again growling. *Be strong, carry on. Slippery slope.* Andrew drove all day and let the street lights escort him deep into the night. His subconscious took the wheel as he was away, in a far off place, fighting urges and demons and twisted thoughts.

6

Surveillance

The lobby was decorated with holly and lights, in the corner stood a seven-foot Christmas tree full of candy canes and pictures of the staff. Cinnamon sticks lay next to the Keurig machine which continually pumped out steaming-hot cider. The atmosphere was most pleasant, aided by the seasonal aroma of pine. Behind the welcome desk were tiny stockings, each one with an employees name on it. The Christmas spirit was alive and well.

"I hate this stupid thing." Stacy said as Andrew entered the lobby laughing.

"Take it off then." He said jokingly, staring at the green and white elf hat atop her head.

"Patty doesn't want me to take it off. - I already asked." Stacy looked pissed. "I look ridiculous!"

"Sorry, but I tend to agree." He said laughing again.

"Shut up." She joked. "There is a supervisors meeting scheduled in a few minutes."

"Alright. Thanks." He said as he stretched into the over-sized white smock and covered his beard.

People seemed to be doing well since the funeral. The staff was upbeat. It was hard to be miserable around Christmas, no matter the situation. Everyone smiled and waved as Andrew headed to the crows nest. The clanking of the steps made it impossible to sneak upstairs unannounced.

"Hey bud." Art said as Andrew entered the supervisors area.

"How's it going Art?"

"It's alright, minus all the fruit cakes coming out flat." Art said a little curious and upset.

"Aren't Fruit cakes usually flat?" Andrew responded with a hint of sarcasm.

"Yeah, but not like this." Art said before he dropped the brick-like fruit cake on the table with a thud. The legs shook. "We can't sell these."

"Oh, just give them to Patty. She wants the defectives." Andrew said with certainty.

"What? Since when? They're suppose to go off to R&D to figure out what's wrong."

"Patty told me a few weeks ago that we changed the flour, shortening and one other thing. Said Baxters had a better product or something."

"Well, it definitely ain't better." Art said as he looked through the file cabinet and pulled out a couple pink slips. He took a quick look and pointed at something. "Cheaper, not better." He looked back at Andrew inquisitively. "Did she tell you in an email?"

"No, in person, why?"

"Cuz your signatures are all over these invoices and PO's. And, I never heard anything from R&D about a change in formula." Art said, with a worried look on his face.

"Well, why-"

"Meetin' time boys, you can finish this *stimulating* conversation later." Lindsay cut them short as he finished his last sip of coffee, then clued them to the door.

Stacy had her hands full. A pitcher of Diet Coke with lemon in her left hand and a thermos of hot coffee in her other.

"Need a hand?" Art asked chivalrously, while holding the door for her.

"No, I'm fine, go on in." She politely declined, as there wasn't enough room to get around him.

They entered. Stacy setting the drinks on the refreshment table, Art and the other supervisors filing in, taking open chairs. There were blank placards in front of them, a few supervisors played with them or doodled on them, trying to determine their importance.

"They want you to put your names on the paper in front of you." Stacy clarified.

Now they were all interested. It wasn't quite the EOQ and EOY yet, and the financial review meeting wasn't scheduled for another six-weeks or so. Although Patty loved meetings, there didn't seem to be an obvious reason for this one.

"Any idea what this is all about?" A supervisor asked.

"Not exactly, but Casey from HR is here, -in the office with Patty." Stacy said quietly, as she saw herself out of the room. The supervisors spoke amongst themselves, some catching up with friends that worked different shifts, others rumoring, others discussing production, and many discussing the mysterious meeting. The room was loud, boisterous.

"Good afternoon everyone. Happy holidays!" A younger man, stylishly dressed, wearing thick, rigid, dark framed glasses that stole attention from his wild dirty-blonde surfer hair, said as he entered the room. He spoke with a warm weathered accent and an intentional lisp. "I'm Casey from the Drury Lane HR team. I haven't had the pleasure to meet you all before, so I put some placards out to help." Patty snuck in behind him and took the seat closest to him. "This place looks and smells amazing! You guys have really made a name for yourself out here." He said, trying to break the ice and build a little rapport.

"Well, I'm sure you're all wondering why I'm here. Don't worry, you're not fired!" The hipster laughed, but should've took the temperature of the room first. The supervisors remained silent, looked around for a social clue, then a couple snickered; not at the joke, at the joker. "Drury Lane Bakeries strategic team has decided to adopt the 'Balanced Scorecard' approach to business." The crowd looked clueless, with the exception of Patty who was obviously introduced to it earlier.

"The Balanced Scorecard helps management by giving equal weight to areas like financials, processes, customers AND workforce...YOU. So, every February we will now be surveying the workers of Drury Lane. The employee engagement surveys give us an idea of your job satisfaction, engagement, your thoughts about upper management and company values...amongst other things." Casey continued. His speech was smooth, well prepared and practiced, but lacked authenticity.

Patty looked apathetic, but if one were to look closer, they might see her legs fidgeting, bouncing around, her hands constantly moving: playing with her hair, clasped in front of her, or tucked under her legs. Andrew understood it all now, she stayed steps ahead of everyone like a chess match. She knew this was coming. *And there it is, you conniving bitch, the real reason. You fake.* Unable to contain her non-verbal clambering, she stood up and walked to the refreshment table to pour a coffee. She looked toward Casey and silently mouthed, 'you want some?'.

"No, I'm fine, thank you. Does anyone need a coffee or one of your amazing muffins?" Casey tried to win some of them over, offering Patty as help. A bunch of hands shot up, not wanting to miss the chance to be waited on by Patty. "Patty", he motioned her to take note of the hands.

"I'll take a coffee and a muffin." Stacy said from the doorway. She smiled and let out a laugh only the supervisors understood.

"Ahhh, Stacy. Come on in, you should be here too. I was just telling everyone about the survey."

"So, how do we take this survey?" Frank asked.

"Good question. An email will be sent to every employee with a company email address, and the rest will have a generic log-in code they can use to log on and take the survey."

"And, who sees these surveys?"

"Okay, well first, its handled by a third party. Then after they collect all the data, they send the results to upper management, at which point you'll be able to see the scores and comments."

"So, if its sent to my email address, won't they know the scores are from me?" Andrew asked, moving his attention from Casey to Patty.

"Excellent question, one I've been asked almost every meeting. No, they will not know it's yours, as long as you leave identifying information out of your comments. The survey is anonymous, otherwise, of course, the scores could be skewed."

The meeting kept on for the next hour as Casey fielded question after question unfazed. The coffee eventually cooled and the muffins hardened, signs the meeting was coming to a close. The power point came to an end, the pointer powered off, and the room buzzed with possibility. Casey had no idea the Pandoras box this survey would unlock, but he liked the excitement in the room. They finally had a voice, and someone to listen.

"Thank you everyone. Very nice to meet all of you." Casey said genuinely, making an attempt to shake everyones hand as they exited the room. The supervisors shook his hand, pleased, not specifically with him but the news. "Merry Christmas."

They all headed back off to check on the production that happened over the past hour. They were jovial and talkative, chit-chatting the rest of the day. The intercom never once crackled, nothing broke their spirit. The swing shift was finishing, people were slipping into their day clothes and winter gear, ready for dinner. They congregated by the time-clock, then filed out the door to the lobby.

"Thank you everyone. Nice work today." Her voice a little tired, but enough energy to feign a plausible amount of sincerity.

"Oh thanks Patty. You're here late." A worker noticed.

"Just making sure everyone's alright."

"Well, good to see you." The worker said while struggling to push the door open against the strong winds. Patty continued to stand in the lobby, thanking the workers, fully committed to her rouse. She would mimic the typical small talk like 'stay warm' or 'drive safe' that she overheard others say, but failed to deliver the feeling. A good ten minutes passed as she noted, while interrogating the clock between every employee. A bundled-up woman knocked on the lobby door from the outside, having left her badge in the car.

"Oh hey-jay-ja" Patty opened the door, and struggled with her name.

"Jessie. Say is that your car out there?" She said pointing at the pristine Lexus with custom plates.

"Yes, why?"

"Well, you may want to look at your drivers side door." Jesse said, a little winded from the run back in the cold weather. The door still cracked, Jesse added, "It's pretty bad," as she headed back off into the snowy parking lot.

Patty walked briskly with intention to her office and grabbed her petticoat. Pulling it on with a little aggravation.

"Everything alright?" Stacy asked noticing a change in her mood.

"Not sure." Patty threw on her matching black earmuffs and scarf, and headed unhappily out the door. She circled the car a few times, standing a few feet from the drivers side, she stomped her feet and turned angrily back toward the lobby. Stacy held the door for her.

"You alright?" Her words vaporizing as they hit the air.

"NO! Someone scratched 'cunt' into my car." She yelled at Stacy. "Who the fuck? It's Christmas for fuck sake." She quieted down as a worker turned the corner to the lobby. She didn't say anything to him, just gave him a second rate smile and made sure he left the building.

"Jeez, I'm sorry. Can you get it fixed?"

"Of course I can get it fixed. I just wanna know who the hell did it." Patty spit at her. "Get me the security cameras from the parking lot." She demanded of her as she stomped off toward her office.

"I can't." Stacy said softly, carefully preparing for the wrath.

"What! What do you mean you can't?" Patty snarled.

"They aren't working anymore." Stacy explained.

"Why?!?!?!"

"Remember after last years review you had me cancel the

service to save on overhead costs."

"Oh." Patty said with slight embarrassment. "Yeah! I re-member! Why didn't you tell me you canceled it then?" She asked, not making sense, just trying to pass the buck. "Forget it...Nevermind!" She slammed her office door, then headed back off into the cold.

"Should I hold your calls?" Stacy laughed as soon as Patty was out of earshot.

7

The Muffin Man

She slammed the door behind her.
[Lost in Space- Aimee Mann]
Motherfucker. Who the hell?
"I worked my ass off for this car. Who do they think they are?" She said aloud to herself. The wind growled against the windshield. She squeezed the leather wrapped steering wheel tight with both hands, her neck and facial muscles tensed until her head started to shake with anger. She slammed the key into the ignition, cranking on the key so long that the starter began grinding on the flywheel.

"Rrrggghh." She let out her aggression, an anger teetering toward sadness. With her eyes welling up, she refocused her angst. *Probably that 'holier than thou' prick. He's been going at me ever since he started. Thinking he's got all the answers since he's in business school.* She yanked the transmission down to drive, the wheels struggled to find traction in the wet sludge. *None of them know. None of them understand.* As she drove down the well-traveled Minnesota highway, people pointed at her door as she blew by them. While waiting at a stoplight, a station wagon pulled into the turn lane parallel to her. Kids were

43

pointing, the flabbergasted father turned, rolled his window down and mouthed something of concern to Patty.

"I know, I know." She hollered at her drivers side window. "God." She screamed, choking back tears. With one hand she dug into her center console, revealing an airplane bottle. Patty cracked the lid with force, threw it back, and yelled at the window again. "What?!?!?" She dropped the bottle at her feet then turned on the radio.

[San Andreas Fault- Natalie Merchant]

The music hit a nerve, and she broke into a heavy sob. *They have no idea how hard I worked to get here. Screw them. How many times I had my ass grabbed, how many times I was called a bitch, a gold digger—40 years.*

"Forty years!" She wailed as the car swerved from the jerk of her hands. Her foot pushed down, her hands wrenched. The Lexus traveling much faster than the forty-five miles per hour posted. Her mind drifted from the windy road ahead her, to the torment of the beatings from her first husband. She cried, and took her foot from the accelerator. The tires rode the curb, slowing to a stop by the side of the road.

Lake Minnetonka typically stayed frozen for three or four months. The icy shores butted up against the roadside, hardly enough shoulder for a car to pass. She grabbed another bottle, her hands shaking, spilling it as it approached her mouth. She worked hard to afford to live on the lake. It was the one place, that she felt free. Work demanded a certain commitment to meet barely attainable goals. The stress placed on her by the executives was impossible to deal with sober, especially with her unique circumstance. She raised the volume on the radio, exited the car carrying a small brown bag and sat on the hood of her Lexus, staring at the street lights across the frozen water.

The songs broke into commercials, and she continued to pull bottles from the bag.

"Ohhh, do you know the muffin man, the muffin man, the muffin man?" The children singing the silly commercial jingle made her twist her body, looking back. She was broken. The jingle continued.

"Oh Harvey, how did you leave me with *this*?" She cried unfettered, looking up at the star filled sky.

The singing stopped, as a mans voice spoke over the jingle. "From a little corner store to a nation-wide bakery. Drury Lane has been proud to serve you for over sixty years. Hi, I'm Harvey Drury, CEO of Drury Lane Bakeries, but you can call me 'The Muffin Man.'" The way the man spoke, he must have had been smiling while they recorded it.

"God," a sad laugh crept into her sobs, "can't they make a new commercial." *He's been dead for three years now.* She gazed across the lake, unbothered by the car horns as they passed her car. He was everything her first husband wasn't; a gentlemen, chivalrous, caring, and terminally ill. Cancer ignored all the good deeds. When she met him he was in his late sixties, his children grown, having children of their own, and his health diminishing. She was an employee for Drury Lane, holding many different positions over the previous thirty years. Then she met Harvey during the annual company awards ceremony. It was her first year as a manager and she was a long way from winning any kind of award. The radio DJ, pulled her back into the night, as he introduced the next song.

[Strong Enough- Sheryl Crowe]

Our wedding song. She fell deeper into hysterics, dreaming about a past long gone. She started thinking about his passing, and how difficult it was. His son, Peter, never liked her, but was decent to her in respect for his father, but since he passed, he treated her terribly. He demanded that she even change her last name back to Claron, but she refused. She loved Harvey, not his money or the company, which is why she was completely comfortable signing the prenuptial agreement. The only thing left to her, the elaborate tomb of a house: six bedrooms, seven bathrooms, a library, a den, an excerise room, a four-season porch, and a five car garage, nestled behind a gate and crop of trees, facing Wayzata Bay.

With Harvey's passing, she was simply an employee of Drury, an employee that the new CEO, Peter Drury, longed to retire and remove. She felt as though she had to earn her job everyday, that she had to impress every chance there was, or she would be gone. Out in the world, alone. She began thinking of what would happen if Peter tossed her away. A woman, sixty-one years-old, no college degree, no work experience other than Drury. *Fuck you Peter.*

"Fuck you Peter." Her thoughts saturated her tongue. She cracked another bottle then walked out onto the frozen lake. The shoreline water was solid, further out it creaked and cracked. "I love you Harvey!" She yelled to the stars. The music from the distant car was barely audible.

There was a hole in the ice ahead of her. She approached it confidently with mascara soaked tears. The airplane bottle flew into the night and it slid across the ice. Her steps at first certain slowly became short and timid. "Fuck you Peter." She whispered as she inched her way toward the hole. She stuck her heeled foot out, wobbling its way into the bone-chilling water. *Why am I still here? What's the reason. Why did you leave me?* She stared at the dark open water, so dark that it did not even reflect the stars; it was abysmal. She knelt toward it. "Fuck you

Andrew." She whispered and took a deep breath.

"Hey, hey. You okay miss?" A concerned motorist shouted, walking toward her from the shore. "Your car break down?" She turned her head toward the man. "You gotta be careful out here, the ice is thin."

"I'm fine." She said plainly and stood up.

"Do you want a hand?" He kindly offered his hand to escort her back to the shore.

"I'm fine." She resisted, pushing his hand away. "Didn't you hear me?" She said with irritation, her face no longer carrying emotion.

"Jeez, okay. Just trying to help." He shook his head, and walked ahead of her back to his car.

She snatched the bag on the hood and got back into the car.

8

Colder Weather

[Colder Weather- Zac Brown Band]

"Maybe tomorrow would be better." She said, not wanting to argue in front of the boys as she round them up. Avoiding eye contact, avoiding the emotion.

"Can I call you then?" Andrew asked, while he helped Christopher with his coat. His throat choked up, his eyes pooled in the corners. The words garbled. "I want to see you again." The words hung in the air, waiting for her to catch them, but she never did.

"Come on boys." She spoke softly, she couldn't give him the answers he wanted. The answers he had to find.

He could still smell her hair, feel her breath. The memory slowly faded, revealing the present moment. The tight leather of the chaise didn't bend or give as he leaned forward.

"That was the last time I saw her." Andrew confessed. "About four months ago."

"Well, I am so glad you have finally started to open up and share. We have made progress. Now, have you tried to speak to her since?" The comfortably dressed professional behind the desk asked him.

"No. She won't talk to me."

"How do you know?"

"I just do. She wrote, 'I hope you find what your looking for' all over our wedding picture." Andrew said recalling the time he came home in a stupor to an empty and quiet house, seeing the crooked picture staring at him unavoidably.

"So, what are you looking for?" The man asked clearly.

"I don't know...happiness?" Andrew said unsure with a half-question, half-statement.

"What do you mean by that?"

"I just want to be happy." Andrew explained simply. "Just be able to smile and mean it. Feel free. Not have my integrity challenged daily."

"And, your wife and kids are keeping you from that?"

"Well, I feel stuck, like I can't breathe."

"Is it because of them?"

"Umm, No, I guess not."

"Well, then what is the reason?" The man felt like he was finally getting to something tangible.

"Probably work, my boss. She is a fucking terrible person.—-oops". He attempted to retract his words, after his anger made him slip. "I'm sorry I didn't mean—."

"No, don't worry, these things are complicated and emotional."

"It's just she has no scruples, she doesn't care about anyone. And it gets under my skin."

"Is it something you are able to deal with? Just let go?" The man asked thoughtfully.

"That's what they all say at work. 'Just let it go'. No one stands up for anything. It pisses me off." Andrew said, getting visibly upset.

"Have you tried to talk to her about it then?"

"No way, she's my boss, she's totally unapproachable. Plus, she's vindictive."

"Sounds like she has issues of her own. Do you ever just think of her as a person and not your boss? A person with their own problems?"

"Well—-"

"Because you know we all have our problems and issues, sometimes it just takes the right person or the right time or situation for them to be solved." He typically didn't interrupt, but needed to add a message that might connect with his patient.

Andrew sat and let the thought marinate. *Would I react to her differently if she wasn't my boss? Does she have problems like I do?* All things he hadn't contemplated before. The psychologist let him go off in his head for a while, but reeled him back in; there were some questions he had to ask.

"So, have you had any alcohol since we last spoke?"

"No, but almost. Something stopped me."

"That's good. What was it that stopped you?"

"Actually it was my boss. I saw her at the liquor store."

"See, she is a human being, with human problems." The connection was perfect and helped him break through to his patient. "Did she see you? Does she know about your legal and marital issues?"

"No she didn't see me. And, I don't think she knows about any of it."

"Hmmm." He thought out loud. "Do you think she should know about it, in case it affects anything at work?"

"I don't see how it's her business. And, I really don't think she'd react well to it."

"Sometimes you can be surprised." He said. "Just give it some thought." He scribbled down a few notes, and grabbed a pad from the desk. "I'm going to write you a prescription for Nortryptaline. It helps with a few things like your morning headaches and feelings of depression. Remember, it doesnt excuse you from facing your issues or dealing with your feelings. Avoidance will only get you deeper. Kay?" He said handing over the script. "Now, what time works best for you for the next appointment?"

They spoke a few moments longer, then exchanged pleas-antries and handshakes. The patient lobby small, but full. A mother and father and child, a woman relegated to a wheelchair, and a self-conscious, Abercrombie teen. *Are they all like me? I'm not the only one, that's good.* He left the appointment feeling better than when he arrived. He felt stronger, proud of his progress. *Maybe I could tell Patty.* His shift didn't start for another hour, enough time to try to talk to his wife.

[Growin' Up- Macklemore and Ryan Lewis]

He sat in the car, the early afternoon sun reflected off the hard snow covering, snuck through the still barren trees and onto the tops of his hands as they rested on his phone. He was happy, confident as he picked up the phone and scrolled to her name. Suddenly he was bombarded by thoughts as if they magically jumped from the name before him on the phone and into his body. The fingers on his other hand raised to his lips as his teeth nervously bit at them. *What if she doesn't answer? Would it be worse if I didn't call or if I called and she didn't answer?* His mind melted from confidence like clocks in 'Persistence of Memory'. He wasn't sad, his strength just wavered. Still trying to figure out how to get back to the life he once had. He grabbed the script from his pocket, examined it and began the ritual of starting the car.

With the windows partially cracked, the cool, brisk air kept him lively, and kept him from falling too far into his thoughts. He drove past a park where children raced parents in toboggans. It scolded him for his dedication to all-things work. Before heading to the bakery, he stopped by the pharmacy and dropped off the prescription. He wasn't fond of the idea of needing help from drugs, but he was to the point where he'd try just about anything, and he was finally starting to trust the psychologist.

From a couple lights away the retro-tin muffin sign adorned with 'Drury Lane Bakeries' in cursive rose above the surrounding buildings. The words his psychologist said stayed with him 'sometimes you can be surprised'. Telling Patty about his issues would leave him vulnerable. *Can I trust her? How will she react?* Although he hated the idea of opening himself up to her, he found it hard to argue with his psychologists logic.

Still early for his shift, he stayed in the car and debated with himself. He began to believe that if he could do this, it could make him much stronger. Maybe even strong enough to reach out to his wife. *Alright!* He attempted to psych himself up. *I can do this! She'll understand, like the psychologist said: she's human.* He strode confidently into the lobby.

"Hey Stacy," he planted his open hands on the counter and leaned in. "Is Patty here?"

"Yeah."

"Is she busy?" He asked, somewhat hoping she was.

"No, just polishing the trophies." She joked. "Why?"

"I need to talk to her about something."

"Should I have the AED ready?" She laughed.

"No." Andrew said waving his hand in dismissal with a little chuckle. "It's actually important."

"Alright, alright. Good luck." Stacy said.

Andrew checked his appearance, tugging on his shirt, making sure it was wrinkle-free and proper. He grabbed the lint roller on Stacys desk and cleaned his pants. He let out a deep sigh, alleviating some tension. *Alright.* His hand rose, paused, then somewhat begrudgingly knocked on her door.

"Come in." A muffled older voice said from inside. He opened the door. "Ah, Andrew. What can I do for you?" She asked nicely with a smile. *Maybe she will surprise me.*

"Hey Patty. Do you have some time?" Andrew's voice tinged with caution.

"Sure, sit down."

"So, I need to tell you something. Uh, umm. Something I probably should have told you before." His voice garbled with emotion. She moved papers from her desk to the table behind her, she allowed him to continue. "Well, I." She was staring at him, he couldn't read her thoughts.

"It's alright go ahead." She got up, shut the door, and sat back down.

"I got a DUI about 4 months ago." Her eyes remained trained on him, unmoved. "Well, it hasn't been settled in court or anything yet. But, I just thought you should know." He let out a bated breath. That was half of it. "And." She sat back in her chair with a look of rumination on her face, eyes still focused on him. "And, my wife left with the kids around that time too. We're currently separated." Still no response. "I just thought, as my boss, you should know what's going on in my life. You know, so you could understand me better." The words flew out of his mouth swiftly. He sat there for a moment, winded but happy with himself.

"Well, thank you for telling me." Still sitting back, the dead pan look slowly mutated to a sly smile. "But, I already knew all of that."

"Oh." Andrew said, caught a little off guard.

[Red Hands (big guitar)- Walk Off the Earth]

"I noticed your license plates in the parking lot." She said openly, as she folded her hands together. Andrews body started to tense. "Then I looked inside and saw the breathalyzer." Andrew started feeling a little light-headed. *What?* "Then, I looked your name up in the public records."

"Oh." He choked. The room began to disappear, the dark edges of his vision started creeping inward. The pace of his breathing had increased exponentially, until he felt the world could hear his exhales through his nostrils. "Oh." His brain began to shut down. "Oh. Oh. Oh." He tried to stand up. His muscles fully tensed and rigid. *Fuck, I.* His sweaty hands slipped from the arm rests, and he stumbled a little. His vision, now a pin point, filled only with Pattys vile smile. His head turned toward the door, only able to see the handle. *Have to get to the door.* He felt like he was crawling on all fours to the door.

"Wait." She said, pointing to the empty chair across from her. "I'm not done." He paused, not turning around, still locked on the door handle.

"Your wife called the other day." *Oh, Jesus Christ.* He couldn't breath now, he started coughing believing it would somehow open his lungs. "Stacy was gone so I answered it." She explained. "I told her you were busy. She told me what was going on. It sounded important. I told her I was sorry but you were still busy." Her voice rumbled through his head, like she was speaking from inside his skull. "Probably shoulda told you." She snickered happily, watching him crumble. "Sounds to me *Andrew*, that *you* should get your shit together." She said standing up from the desk. Andrews hands fumbled about, hitting the door, the file cabinets next to the door, everything but the door handle. *Get out Andrew.*

"Oh. Oh. I." His limp hand fell on the handle. Andrew tumbled out of the office and crawled to the wall, bracing himself up. His breath erratic, he could feel his thready pulse pound throughout his whole body. The hallway continued to shrink. *JESUS, HELP! SOMEONE HELP ME!* He couldn't speak, his body on the verge of total shut down.

"Andrew!" Stacy screamed as she ran from behind her desk, after hearing his body hit the floor. Patty walked calmly over to the door, saw the two huddled against the wall, then closed the door.

"I. I." He gasped. "I can't breathe."

"You're having a panic attack." She sat across from him, holding his hand. "Listen to my voice, feel my breathing." She continued talking quietly, and placed his hand over her chest. "It will be alright. Just listen to my voice. Feel my breathing." She repeated.

Surprise.

9

Persona Non Grata

[Otherside (remix)- Macklemore and Ryan Lewis]

The front door blasted open, swinging in violently from a boot. The house empty, dark, other than the cardboard boxes stacked against the couch, garbage bags strewn across the kitchen and the dim light that crept in from the street lights. *Son of a bitch.* A beautiful young woman in all white and a gangly young man in black stared at him from a distant wall. *Stop smiling! How can you be so happy?* Andrew trooped over to the fridge, from the cupboard above it his hand seized a bottle without discrimination. The earlier incident with Patty completely wiped out his inhibitions, allowing the charlatans in his head to take control. He twisted the cap, with nothing and no one to stop him he finished the bottle, which then clanked against the stainless steel of the sink. His throat tingled, feeling arid and dry. *Not enough.*

Inside the dark, warm fridge was a torn case of Milwaukees Best, ketchup, cat food, spoiled milk and a notebook. He fisted a beer and slammed the notebook on the cheap, derelict foldout card table in the middle of the vinyl floor. The smell of hot beer twisting in his sinuses didn't slow his pace. Three beers later he pulled out the folding chair, when he sat he was rudely reminded of the pill bottle in his back pocket. He fumbled with the top a minute then divvied out four pills.

"Why didn't you listen to me? I told you she was evil. I told you." His words wet with alcohol. "But, no, no, no, it's just in my head. I'm *too* sensitive." He jammed an index finger into his temple, and strangled the hot beer, the aluminum crunching in his fist. He cocked his hand back. The picture frame crashed to the floor covered in the rancid odor of cheap beer. *I love you.*

He retreated to the deep corners in his mind, searching for that locked closet where he believed his creativity was held captive. His liver couldn't keep up. He was inundated by thoughts from everywhere, everytime. The pen moved faster than his mind, the words like darts, lucky if they hit the target.

One by one the pills vanished from beside his notebook. *If one is good, two is better, right? I'm not ignoring my thoughts doc.* His intoxicated mind tried but failed to rationalize and give credence to his actions, but something in him still actually believed his drinking was justified, remembering what the psychologist said about ignoring his problems. *Screw it.* He chased the last pill with more warm beer. The self-pity began to outpace his anger. His writing mellowed, until it bled with a rank woefulness.

Drowsiness settled in, he ambled to the bathroom, flicking the light switch numerous times to no avail. The house dark and his vision blurred, he was forced to use his phone to light the toilet as he took aim. Foul piss slapped the ring, struggling to find water, he accidently pissed on his hand, his other hand dropping the phone in reaction. The phone sinking, illuminated the toilet from the bottom, he continued to urinate.

"Shit." He said only mildly bothered, with a look of 'ho-hum' on his drunken face. He turned to the sink and waited for the water to warm, but it never did. *Damn.* He splashed the cold water on his face, the pungent smell of urine still locked into the pores of his hands. *Pathetic.* Scrutinizing himself in the mirror, he picked at his patchy, stray beard and rubbed his sunken, bloodshot eyes.

The remainder of the night was roughly the same: more beer, more writing, more vulgarity, more tears, more slurring, more piss. Around the time the lights outside his abandoned home went out, he ambled to the bedroom, using the walls to brace him, crashing fully-clothed, on top of the comforter-less California king.

The blinds did nothing to subdue the late-morning sun, light peering through each slat at the miserable man splayed out across the bed. A fly hung from the ceiling fan blade, he looked down upon himself. *What a detestable creature.* His eyes temporarily stunned and paralyzed as his pupils recoiled and reduced to the size of a pin head. Morning headaches persisted in spite of the medication, and his body ached, weary from the lack of REM sleep. He slipped from the bed, disrobing in preparation for his cold awakening.

The pipes had yet to freeze but it felt like ice to Andrew, luckily in Minnesota it was illegal for them to shut off his gas in the winter, which meant the house was still warm. Unfortunately, the water heater was electric. The pores across his skin tightened, his weakened body was shocked into a lively state. He yanked the shower curtain out of his way and grabbed the soiled, unwashed towel caked with months of dead skin. Motivation was absent as he struggled to finish his morning routine. He felt disgusted with himself as he passed the depressing display in the kitchen. His friendly house fly settled in the folds of his ear. Swatting recklessly and never connecting, he only injured himself. *Go away you irritating insect.*

A slight worry was developing when he was unable to find his car keys. He tossed the discards of last night around, digging through a pile of clothes, investigating the house, still no keys or phone. Ready to call off the search, he paced before the fridge debating on grabbing a beer to soothe his hangover woes.

"Go away!" He screamed after the hellacious, omnipotent buzzing. With his hand in the beer case about to give in, he found them. *The keys.* His fingers moved from the beer to the keys. *Not now.*

The snow covered car started right up at the conclusion of his routine. Driving to work was painful, between his headache, nausea, body ache, and his eyes reaction to the light he was an absolute wreck. He almost felt more drunk than hung over, but somehow alcohol wasn't detected during his little routine. The radio blared commercials, the volume left at the previous levels from last nights angry music, his head couldn't handle it. As he went to adjust the volume he saw the time. *Shit.* Twelve thirty-six, at this rate he'd only be two hours late to work. *Why didn't my alarm go off?* He patted his pockets and looked around his car. *Where's my phone?* He spent the whole ride fretting about Patty's reaction to his tardiness.

"Good *afternoon.*" Stacy said stressing the afternoon. "You don't look so good."

"Yeah, I feel like crap." Andrew mumbled while he pulled on his white smock. "Rough night."

"Well, for one, I'm surprised your car started." Patty burst out of the office having seen him pull up. "I mean with that breathalyzer thing and all. You'll be staying late a few hours tonight now, correct?"

"Sure." How could he argue, he was late, and it was absolutely his fault.

"Before you go do whatever it is that you do, go get me those fruit cakes and put them in the boxes in my office." Patty said walking back into her office. Andrew nodded obediently.

"Remember it's the year end meeting today." Stacy said, then looked at the clock. "Peter should be here in an hour or so."

"Oh god, I forgot." He said, totally oblivious.

"Don't worry, I have printed out the numbers for everyone. You should be able to BS your way through it."

"Thanks. Better go get those cakes." Andrew said placing the net over his patchy, oily, unkempt beard. The incessant buzzing had him tugging and rubbing his ears.

The staff all looked at him, analyzed him. Some said 'tisk, tisk' rubbing their index fingers across each other. Others shook their head, easily able to determine the reason for his tardiness. He worked his way across the floor to the rarely used storage room outside the three-story freezer. Flicking on the lights revealed a neatly stacked pallet of fruit cakes; nine by nine by five high. He wheeled the pallet as close to Patty's office as possible, then began hauling them by hand.

"Stack them nicely." She said pointing to the boxes in the corner.

He finished unloading the cakes, then made his way up to the crows nest.

"He lives!" Art said, his nose riled. "And, he smells like he had a little too much fun."

"Thanks." Andrew responded with half a smile, then pulled on his collar to smell his clothes. "Whatever."

"You ready for the meeting?" Troy asked.

"Not really, but we all know what Patty likes to hear."

"Yeah, production up, cost per unit down, labor down." Art and the rest of the supervisors said robotically in unison. "Even if it's not completely true." Art added. "You see that nice stack of fruit cakes yet?"

"Yeah, she had me box them up for her right when I got here."

"Good thing you weren't *too* late then." Art snickered.

"What do you mean by that?"

"Well, I think I figured out why she had you change the products." He paused, Andrew looked at him to continue. "Remember at the end of last quarter she said we needed to make up a dollar or so in cost per unit." Andrew nodded. "And, she said if we didn't figure something out, she would....well, I think she figured it out. And." Art emphasized. "And, If anything goes sideways she's got you holding the bag." He said waving the POs, and pink invoices. The defects were in the hundreds, but the difference in price between the products they were suppose to use and the ones Patty had directed Andrew to order was more than enough to make up a dollar in cost per unit.

"The scape goat." Frank chimed in on the conversation.

"That's why she had me remove those cakes from the floor?" Andrew asked, scratching his scalp through his hairnet, somewhat knowing the answer.

"Yeah, so Peter wouldn't see them during his inspection. Hence, not *too* late." Art explained, the rest of the room quiet as they let Andrew soak it in.

"Lindsay's last CTOs today!" Troy said, trying to renegotiate the path of the conversation. Lindsay started at Drury not long after returning from Vietnam, he had been with the company for almost as long as Patty and was well versed in her escapades. For the last few years Lindsay became very hands off with pretty much everything involving work, seemingly attempting to severe all attachments, so that the transition to retirement was easier. Andrew's work ethic was polar opposite, he cared too much, and was never able to sever his attachments to work.

"Lucky bastard." Andrew said, as Lindsay hacked out a phlegmy laugh.

"Might be yours too, little shit." He joked through his mustache. The whole room enveloped in laughter. "Seriously though." He spoke a little quieter. "I'd watch what you say around her. She'll throw you under the bus in a heartbeat."

"Yeah." Frank said, removing his hairnet and combing his silver mane back tight. "Lindsay has ten years of tire tracks on his ass." The room roared, only to interrupted by a feigned friendly voice over the intercom.

"Good Afternoon staff, If I could please have all supervisory staff report to the conference room for CTO's. Thank you." She had switched to kiss ass, impress-mode. The CEO was most likely in the office with her. She managed to sound thoughtful.

"Good afternoon......Thank you." Frank mimicked Patty's tone and inflection and dressed it up with kissy sounds. His lead role in a community theater production had Frank deluded into believing he was more charismatic and polished than he actually was. "Oh, I love all of you."

"Well, let's get this over with." Lindsay said.

10

Glorified

He sauntered in behind Patty, and flanked by Larkin the VP of Operations. [Sympathy for the Devil- Rolling Stones] His Canali cream khaki twill suit livened up with a lavender tie and matching pocket square. The fragrance-free policy did not apply to him, his boldly masculine cologne was overpowering.

Peter was known for his aloof style that separated himself from every other executive at Drury. Andrew noticed his handshake was firm and quite inline with his style; his platinum and diamond Piaget watch always peeking out from under his plaid cuffs and monogrammed cufflinks to remind one of their meager status. His pursuit of power and money was second to none; including Patty. Whenever around Patty he always went out of his way to make her shrivel up and seemingly disappear.

He calmly waited for everyone to sit down, gently rubbing his hands together, then once all were seated he carefully pulled out his chair from the closet. The chair was only to be used by Peter, handcrafted in Italy, the leather stitching must have taken months. He had something similar in each of the bakeries across the nation. Just one of the many organizational changes since he took over for his father.

"Looks like you've all worked hard enough to get Patty a chair almost as nice as mine....kudos." Peter adjusted his watch then cuffs, then looked across the table and winked at Patty.

"A car too." One of the supervisors said with some apprehension. Patty threw him a stink eye, then retreated back to analyze her boss' reaction.

Peter stood up from his chair and peered out the bay of windows that faced the parking lot.

"That thing?" Peter asked jovially, noticing the Lexus in Patty's reserved spot. "I bought my daughter one for her sweet sixteen." He mocked, pulling down his jacket as he sat back down in the chair. "Anyway...lets get to it." He nodded to Larkin, who pulled the projection screen down. Larkin hardly ever said anything, his role was more fill than function. A man who would rather be behind the scenes than behind the eight ball; he knew his place. The screen lit up with a bunch of charts and numbers, some red some black, some in italics some bold. Larkin handed Peter the red pointer.

"Well, it all boils down to this." Peter ran the pointer around a number at the bottom of the screen. "Somehow....*somehow*...you did it." He strangely accentuated the second somehow.

Patty grinned happily and leaned in. CTO, contribution to overhead, meetings typically began with a run down of how each division within the bakery performed, explained by the supervisor assigned to the particular division. None of the supervisors were very fond of these meetings, so having Peter jump down to the overall performance was a happy diversion from the norm.

"Lots of hard work, few defects, and no overtime." She

explained. *Nothing to bitch about now Peter.*

The supervisors were all thinking the same thing. *No overtime? At least none we got paid for.*

"Not bad, not bad." Peter allowed her the allotted moment of pride. "You know, the way things ended third quarter, I thought I might have a legitimate reason to fire you at this meeting. But, somehow, somehow, you met or exceeded all the yearly numbers." Peter wouldn't let her enjoy the moment too long without a jab.

"Uh-huh." Larkin cleared his throat, which garnered Peters attention as he moved to the next slide.

"We did, however…" Peter paused as he pointed at the cost accounting notes for fourth quarter. "Have a little discrepancy." Patty's pride crawled underneath the table. "Accounting flagged a couple items where the costs fluctuated rather wildly." The pointer moved to the words, 'Flour, Baking Soda, and Shortening'. "When they looked into it further, they found that the product numbers were different than the ones approved by R&D. Now…"

Patty shifted about in her chair, a bead of sweat pinched and perched in the creases of her brow. Her jowls moved sideways, her teeth running back and forth against each other. The weight shifted in her stilettos quickly from her toes to her heels as she pushed herself up from the table. She looked a mix of nauseous, nerves, and burning rage.

"Andrew ordered some cheap generic brands over the last month or so. I didn't find out, myself, until I started reviewing the PO's and invoices." She blurted, then dug into her masculine attache briefcase, pulling out a few colored slips and sliding them on the table. Patty glared at Andrew with a look that said, 'You say anything, I'll eat your kids.' Peter gave the papers a once over.

"Is this true?" Peter rubbed his cheek, and scratched his sideburn. No response, as Andrew's body entered fight or flight mode, heavily leaning toward flight. "Andrew, is this true?"

"Uh." The question banged through his ear like a snare drum in a marching band. He looked at Patty, still standing, then back toward the CEO. "Umm. Ye—-yeah—-I guess." The fluorescent lights felt as though they began emitting intense heat, and the holes in the ceiling tiles started pulsating in size. *Whats happening?* The pace of his breathing quickened.

"He, he" Patty started, Peter interrupted.

"It's alright Patty. I've got this." Peter stood up and walked around the table. All eyes were on Andrew's face, but to him they were a giant blur. He began to fidget with his collar, coughing a little.

Peter was now directly behind Andrew, placing his hands on the back of the chair.

"This...gentlemen." Peter intentionally left ladies out. "This is forward thinking. This is dedication to the bottom-line." Peter patted Andrew on his shoulder. The intensity of the situation bottomed out. Patty turned white as a ghost. "This is what I expect out of you Patty. This young man, might be taking your job if you aren't careful."

Andrew was silent, still in the thralls of panic. His mind somewhere distant, slowly making its way back. The supervisors painfully restrained their laughter.

"But...but he." Patty stammered, her words difficult to find.

"No Patty. *No!* If it weren't for this young mans initiative you'd be out of a job. So, I'd carefully choose your words." Peter moved from Andrew's chair toward Patty, pointing a hard stiff finger. "I don't believe there is much more to discuss." He turned about and circled the table to his chair, where his hands gripped the taut deep brown leather. "Except maybe have this up-and-comer attend the annual awards to accept the best Cost Per Unit award. He earned it." He shoved the chair, rolling it toward Patty.

Peter adjusted his coat and cuffs, then exited the room and the building with Larkin in tow. Patty scrambled to pick all the papers up from the table, shoving them angrily and urgently into her briefcase. She looked on the verge of a mental breakdown, but no one was concerned enough to lend a hand. Andrew's mind still off in a far away land, his body reacted and sorted the papers of the table in front of him.

"Get your fucking hands off of them!" Patty smacked his hand and grabbed the papers. "You, you...you," she couldn't choose between the combination of insults dancing in her head. Once the table was cleared, she hurried off, her heels catching the door threshold she fell to a knee, holding tight to her attache case to secure the incriminating papers. Once the latch of her office door clicked the conference room lit up.

"Oh my god dude, that was amazing!" Troy said, displaying his youth.

"Seriously, Peter made Patty his bitch." Frank laughed, fixing his non-existent cuff links, then pulled a comb from his pocket. Years of pent-up aggression, they finally had the opportunity to rejoice in the pain administered to their nemesis.

"Whoa." Art said, in utter amazement. "How bout that Andrew?" Art nudged an elbow into Andrews side, nothing. "Andrew?"

"Hey, pal?" Lindsay kicked Andrew from across the table, it jarred him from limbo; the place between Wayzata and the nether regions. He reacted with a shudder.

"Oh, yeah. That was crazy." Andrew said, hoping it was an acceptable reaction to the conversation he missed.

As he walked the floors of the bakery, random staff members came up to him, patted his back and offered congratulations. It was as though he had saved the town from a fire-breathing dragon. Andrews emotions were everywhere, and he still felt a little drunk or hung-over, he couldn't tell the difference. The entire first half of his shift he was choking down vomit, his mouth burning from the acid, making his atrocious breath unavoidable. After lunch he spent a good ten minutes on his knees hugging the toilet, his stomach churning from nerves and beer. *She's really gonna be gunning for me now...and it wasn't even my fault...she fucked herself over.* The irony of the whole situation was comical, but he couldn't muster a laugh without feeling the urge to throw up.

"Hey kid." The old man tugged on Andrews smock and motioned him away from prying eyes. "Have a couple of these." Lindsay discretely tapped out a couple breath mints into Andrew's palm. "It's foul buddy, and that's coming from a guy that used to drink a bottle of Beam every night."

"Thanks." Andrew tried to speak out the side of his mouth, angling his breath away from the old man. "I've been having some hard times." He shoveled the mints into his mouth.

"Don't I know it. You need a better way to cope kid." His honesty was welcomed, but hard to hear. "Come on over after work. I'll show you how I've learned to deal with that old crow." Andrew was a little taken aback by the bitterness in his tone and choice of words, as he had rarely heard the chain smoker say anything all too negative before.

"Yeah, 'guess it couldn't hurt." Andrew nodded with appreciation. "Thanks. I'll wait for you in the parking lot."

After shift change, Andrew dressed down and headed out to his car. An unusually warm morning made a vague promise that it quickly rescinded. Winter had an encore. The temp not low enough for snowflakes but not high enough for rain. Wet sleet ran sideways, covering the parking lot in a light grey sludge. Andrew's Saturn pulled up alongside the old red Chevy truck which held itself together with bungee cords, a 'cold dead hands' bumper sticker, a wooden gun rack, and rusty steel. The only things in decent condition on the truck were the brand new tires and mud flaps. Lindsay cranked down the window, a cigarette hanging from his lips.

"Come on!" Lindsay said, trying to speak through the sleet and over the loud, fast *wush, wush* of his windshield wipers.

Not a freeway or even a four-lane highway all the way there. Lindsay traveled at a leisurely forty to forty-five miles an hour, allowing the observant driver an opportunity to see and feel the calm of the country roads. What was once dust, now a yellowish muck, spun up from the trucks rear wheels as it entered a gravel road with nothing worthy of note for a considerable distance. Ahead, off to the left, a beige trailer began to materialize through the sleet. The Chevy drove up a slight incline finally coming to a stop under a hard wood tree, the ground below it bare with tire tracks suggested that this was where the Chevy rested on most nights. Lindsay waved him up and over, kicking his boots against the porch steps to dislodge the sludge that accumulated in the treads.

"So this is home?" Andrew asked as he approached, his head bent attempting to avoid the blowing frozen rain.

"This is home. Come on in. Coffee? Coke? Shot a Jack?"

"Thought you said I needed a better way to cope?" Andrew

responded curiously.

"A shot. That's all I ever need. Probably not a drop in the bucket compared to what you did last night. Moderation." Leaving Andrew with a coy, pants-down, look on his face.

"Is that the trick? Your key to coping with Patty."

"Yeah, that and pumping buckshot into watermelons." Lindsay laughed, Andrew joined. "No, I'm serious. You ever felt the kickback of a Mossberg?" He asked not leaving time for a reaction. "Or seen a watermelon explode? It's therapeutic, I swear."

"Naw. Nope. Not a fan of guns." Andrew said almost proudly.

"How would ya know if ya never shot one?" Lindsay said as he poured them a shot and gave one to Andrew, raising it for a toast. "Lets pop that cherry! I'll let you draw Patty's face on the watermelon."

[Glorified G- Pearl Jam]

The two spent the remaining hours of daylight out in the clearing behind the trailer. The snow around a stack of timbers about fifty yards down range was stained pink from a constant splattering of watermelon innards. Andrew was still hesitant, even after watching Lindsay load, grip, pump, aim and unload the shotgun multiple times. The grounds were scattered with green rinds, red cartridges, and grey pellets. Lindsay placed the unloaded shotgun down carefully, and re-entered the trailer. A moment or so later, he returned with yet another watermelon and a black marker.

"Your turn, young buck." Lyndsey handed over the items to his young friend. "Have at it."

Andrew scribbled a crude face upon the melon, then placed the melon on the wood pile. Lindsay began a tutorial on how to carefully load and hold the shotgun. He talked about how to adjust aim with the length of the shot, about smoothly squeezing the trigger and how to absorb the following kickback. It was now time, the gun was loaded and the watermelon effigy waited. The black steel of the shotgun was deathly cold from the winter weather, Andrew's fingers were almost numb as they curved around the trigger. He was unsure how to feel, for all his life, he hated the thought of guns, but now that it was in his own hands it felt different. Staring down the barrel, paring it with the face of Patty, gave Andrew some level of calm. Off the staging area, Lindsay waited, leaning against an old post, tapping out a new cigarette, while one quickly turned to ash between his cold lips.

"Give her hell." Lindsay encouraged him.

Andrew took a deep breath, slowly released it and pulled the trigger. The effigy was complete, the melon eviscerated. Before the blunt force of the kickback even registered, Andrew had destroyed his nemesis, and an awkward smile stained his face.

"Not bad right?" The old man said, looking down range at where the watermelon once resided, now knowing his therapy had worked.

"Not bad at all." Andrew said, holding his shoulder after he placed the shotgun down carefully. "Not bad at all. Can I do it again?"

11

Hollywood

"Did you see him?" Troy asked, giddily. He and Art were leaving the break room.

"No, heard about him though."

"You *gotta* see him." Troy told Art. Art rolled his eyes and adjusted his belt, continuing on the path to the crows nest. "No, really, you gotta." Troy grabbed the back of Art's white smock and renegotiated the route.

They strode across the production facility, around the giant ovens, muffin depositors and cookie conveyor. Off the central production area was the cake decorating room, typically they were the only males that entered this room. A poor excuse for music was blaring from an archaic tape player. A mix of Def Leopard, Van Halen, and many other bands who played the same three chords and sounded just as terrible as the last. The majority of the woman had ear plugs in or attempted to tune it out by concentrating more deeply on their decorating.

"There he is." Troy pointed to the greasy, long haired, middle aged man; with dark eyes and fat, fuzzy caterpillars for eyebrows which were partially covered by the bright red bandana tied around his head. His uniform sleeves rolled up around his biceps, the embroidered name read 'Mitch'.

"What's up Hollywood?" Troy said excitedly.

"Ahhh, *hey* man!" The man in the bandana spoke over the boombox. "Not much, just living the dream man." He laughed turning down the volume. "Cake, frosting and rock and roll!"

"What you making today?" Troy said, partially forgetting the reason he was there. "Oh, this is Art. He's also a supervisor here."

"Ahhh, yeah dude. Pleasure man, pleasure." The man Troy called Hollywood said looking at Art, pulling his bandana a little tighter, then offering a handshake. "Sweet, sweet frosting my man."

"So, how do you like the job Mitch?" Art asked while shaking his hand.

"Hollywood, *Hollywood*. Please man, call me Hollywood." The time-traveler said. "It's great man. Jamming out with the *layyyydies*...YEEAAAHH!" He screamed like his favorite bands did, as he panned his open hand, palm up; as if offering them his harem.

"Alright. Keep up the good work." Art was not entertained, interested or impressed.

"Man, you guys should stop by tomorrow." The poor entertainer said.

"Why?" Troy asked.

"Makin' pie crusts." He said while fiddling with the tape player, a click, a whir, another click. "Cherry Pie!" The hairball song by the same name burst from the twenty year old speaker cones. He laughed and began singing along, head bobbing, making the shaka sign as the supervisors began back toward the door.

"Jesus Christ." Art said.

"I told you. I told you." Troy was hysterical, almost bent over with laughter outside the cake room. "Hollywood." He chuckled.

"Pathetic. Really, more pathetic than funny." Art shook his head with displeasure.

"Oh come on you old fart." Troy gave him a knock in the shoulder. "Lighten up a little."

"Did he take the survey yet?" Art asked Troy, referring to the annual employee engagement survey.

"No, hasn't worked here long enough. Patty wants anyone whos been here more than three months to take it."

"Well, I still have a few people to send over there to take it. Like always she's pestering me to get it done. She wants to be the bakery with the highest percent surveyed." Art explained.

"I know, everything is a contest. Even when it's *not* a contest." The younger supervisor responded in a snarky tone.

"Zero sum game." Art said frankly.

"What?" Troy said naively in a timid voice.

"For someone to win, someone has to lose. No in-between, and definitely only one winner. And, its got to be her. Everytime."

Just as he finished explaining to the high school drop-out the intercom blared.

"Art, please send your remaining employees to my office to finish the survey." Patty chirped, everyone but Art ignored the voice.

"See!" Art said, pointing toward the closest speaker.

"I'll let you get to it." Troy excused himself, allowing the pear shaped supervisor to attend to his business. Art squeezed his portly belly between some cooling racks looking for the three remaining employees of his, yet to take the survey.

"Char!" Art yelled over the ovens, conveyors, and exhaust system. "Char." He finally caught her attention and leaned in. "You need to take the survey. It's in Patty's office. I'll send Rosalinda over to fill in for you here, then she can take it when you're done." He said as he held the oven door open for the homely woman, while she pulled out the hot rack with heavy duty oven mitts. Char was short for Charlotte, but others thought it was short for charcoal, as her teeth looked like she'd been chewing on a briquette all day. "Kay?"

"Yeah, thanks." She leaned closer to Art, handing him the oven mitts.

While Art moved the cake rack to the cooling room, Char walked to the breakroom; removed her protective gear, washed her hands and headed to Patty's office.

"Hello Char." Patty took a stab at the name, with three left and two with Hispanic names the odds were decent. "How are you?"

"Hi Patty, I'm good. It's hot down there today." Char, the forty year old bachelorette, married to three dogs responded, wiping forming sweat from her forehead.

"Oh, I'm sorry. I'll look into that while you take the survey." Patty told the worker what she wanted to hear. "Do you know what the survey is for?"

"Yeah, kinda, everybody has told me about it already." Char grinned exposing a mouthful of rotting or missing teeth. Patty cringed.

"Okay, good. Well, please feel free to respond, or write whatever you feel, or any concerns you have. Here, you can take my chair, and I'll set it up for you." Patty stood from her chair, and offered it to her. She really played into the needs and wants of her staff, hoping to buy or con them into good results. "Oh, and when you're done with the survey please take a fruit cake or two from the box for you to bring home."

"Oh, how nice. My dogs will love it." Char's laugh whistled through the gaps in her teeth.

"Yes, yes. I'm sure they will." Patty was beginning to feel a need for a bath, having to be around these people. "Now…" She said very nicely and motioned toward the chair. Char sat down, Patty showed her how to take the survey. "I'll be right here for a minute or so if you have any questions." Patty stood directly behind her, in clear view of the screen.

"I'm sure I'll be fine. Thanks." Char said, and Patty reluctantly began to exit the room. "And, thanks again for the fruit cakes." She said cheerfully. Patty smiled disgustingly then kept on her previous path.

Ugh, white trash, almost as bad as the 'no speakas'. Can't believe I have to deal with these…these…losers. Patty thought back to all the years she worked on the production floor as a young woman, back before it was all immigrants, back when it was a decent, respectable way to earn a living. Now, at least in her eyes, it was flooded with the untalented and unwanted; all working merely for a paycheck, with no ambition to go beyond. When she had to stroll the production floor for a Gemba walk, or when she had to speak directly with a line worker it made her skin crawl. Having cheap labor was a necessary evil, and critical to the success of the bakery, and even more directly to Patty's continued employment. Thus, she had to deal with it, no matter how much it bothered her.

"Hi Patty, shall I RSVP your spot for the annual business award meeting?" Stacy drew her away, temporarily, from her thoughts.

"Yes, please. And, get me a driver, I won't be taking my Lexus in that neighborhood." Patty spoke, referencing downtown Minneapolis, and the people that typically frequented the streets.

"Absolutely. And, congratulations on the award."

"Uhhh. Sure." Patty tried to brush off her compliment, unsure if it was sarcastic. "Did you draw up that corrective action form?"

"For Andrew?" Stacy asked with a slight hitch, while Patty gave her the 'of course you idiot' look. "Yes, it's in your mailbox."

"Let me know when, or if, he shows. With as many tardies as he has piled up lately, I'm sure he's debating on whether or not to even show up anymore." Patty said scanning the parking lot for the whiskey plates. "That or he's drunk. —Did you see his license plates?"

"Uh." Stacy started, but was unsure how to answer.

"Nevermind. Just send him to my office, you may have to pick him up off the floor again." Patty said with a cruel wit. "He's too damn sensitive. Grow some balls." Patty finished her tirade as Stacy pointed to something behind her.

"All finished Patty." Char said with a five-toothed smile.

"Oh, thank you so much Char. I see you remembered the fruit cakes." Nodding to the four cakes, two in each hand. *I said two you selfish, snaggletoothed bitch.*

"Ah, yeah. The dogs will love them."

"Take care, Stacy is looking into the heat down there." Patty said as she tapped on Stacy's desk and gave her a clandestine wink. Stacy responded with a look of confusion that quickly turned to 'aha, yes'.

"Thanks Patty, you're the best." Char said with genuine emotion. *Yes, I am.* Char placed two of the cakes under her armpit and extended a hand to Patty in appreciation. Patty reluctantly shook the sad ladies hand.

"Hand me that sanitizer." Patty asked Stacy as soon as Char left for the floor. She pumped a few spots of gel into her hands and rubbed them vigoursly. *I need a bath now.* "I'll be in the office, if Rosalina or that other one come for the survey send them in."

The boxes of fruit cake were almost empty, but even if she had some left they'd keep for years.

According to the linked website, which Patty visited many times a day, there were only a couple of employees that had yet taken the survey, Andrew being one of them. The next closest bakery still had twelve surveys left with the window closing in just a few hours. *Ahhh, first place, again.* The office was quiet enough to hear the second hand jump from number to number which fought only the 'tap, tap' of Patty's Underwood pen on the polished desk. Her eyes fixed on the clock face. *2:15, he's late.* She shoved herself away from the desk, spun around, checked the mailbox, spun back around and pulled back up to the desk; all in one quick aggravated motion. The skin around her knuckle lost color as she crushed the pen between her index and thumb, scribbling her signature across the bottom of the formal letter.

"If he shows up, give this to him." Patty said to Stacy as her hand shot out with the paperwork, her voice over-flowing with ire. "Have him sign it. I'm not waiting anymore."

"Oh—-kay, I guess." Stacy folded. *Put your six hours in huh.*

12

Systemic

The butterscotch candy clicking against his therapist's teeth was driving him crazy. Andrew was already upset with the psychiatrist as his previous suggestion to speak to Patty backfired, to say the least. He was now only half interested in anything the comfortably dressed man in loafers had to say. The crocheted cardigan and his smooth, soft voice drew terrible comparisons to a childrens' television show. This only drew Andrew further away from the conversation. Most went in one ear and out the other, with only drastically over-used jargon staying for any length of time.

"Let's bring it back into the room." The man across the desk said, trying to calm his patient down as he realized his words weren't connecting with his thoughts.

"I mean, did you really think it was gonna work?" Andrew argued in a harsh tone. "She treated me like garbage, didn't even think twice about criticizing me."

"Like I mentioned before. I'm sure she has her own issues. We all—"

"I don't care if she has issues, I just don't want to get treated like garbage." Andrew retorted, finding his therapists answer unacceptable. The psychiatrist began to explain and rationalize the situation, Andrew wanted nothing to do with it. "I'm gonna fix this one way or another. I can't just sit back and watch her destroy everyone else's lives."

"Do you think upper management is aware of her misdeeds?"

"I'm sure. And, I'm sure they don't care unless it negatively affects their bottom line."

"Well, then is it more of a problem with Patty or is it deeper; a systemic issue with the company?"

"Doesn't matter. Whatever it is I'm gonna do something about it...If you don't stand for something, you'll fall for anything."

"Interesting." The shrink said tapping the notepad with his pen. "Do you know who said that?"

"Yeah, Malcolm X."

"And, Alexander Hamilton...do you know what they have in common?"

"No."

"They both died on principle at the hands of their adversary. Are you subconsciously saying you're willing to sacrifice yourself?"

"If that's what it takes." Andrew responded honestly as the concerned psychologist wrote some more notes down. The conversation was set aside for a while as the doctor thought about how best to address the disconcerting issue that grew before him.

"Are you aware that all actions have consequences? -Some intended, others unintended. How do you think your sacrifice would affect your children, your wife?" He asked his patient. The long pause before his response made it obvious that he had not thought about it.

"I don't know. But, at least they had a father who stood up for righteousness."

"Yes, but do you think they'd rather have a father or a tombstone? I'm just trying to get you to think of how all this affects everyone in your life. You aren't alone; this isn't a vacuum."

Shaking his head and blowing out an overdue breath, Andrew's eyes connected with anything but the person talking to him. "Shit, it's past two. She's gonna kill me." Andrew caught a glimpse of the silent, large faced clock.

"She'll understand, it's an important step in your recovery, and if you remember, it's now court mandated, she has to respect that."

"You *don't get it*. Jesus. She'll crucify me." Andrew rushed out of the sparsely decorated office. All the excitement and positivity he felt when he left his last session seemed like a story from someone else's life. All he could feel now was frustration. The people that filled the lobby, the same that had before, now looked pitiful, dispirited, and emotionally crippled. He pushed his way through.

He slammed the car door and angrily blew into the breathalyzer, a beep signaled it was not ready. He blew again, getting the same beep. Andrew yanked the corded breathalyzer around, pounding it against his steering column. It beeped again.

"FUCK!" It beeped again. "Come on damn it." He exhaled long and hard, it blinked green and gave the ready chirp. "Finally." The car started up just before his eyes birthed a tear of futility. Not once during the trip to work did he check the speedometer, not once did his fingers loosen their stranglehold upon the steering wheel, not once did Andrew think about anything related to driving. His anxiety was building, he could feel a throbbing ball of tension where his heart used to be. The Saturn sped into the parking lot, front wheels spinning wildly as the SUV whipped around.

"I'm sorry, I'm sorry. My appointment ran late." Andrew was barely able to get it out between his short, shallow breaths. He looked to Stacy. "Is she here?"

"No, she left for the day, another appointment. She did want me to give you this though." Stacy handed over the 'corrective action' forms.

"Guess I don't really have an excuse not to sign them." Andrew said regrettably disappointed in himself and slightly angry with his psychiatrist. He signed the forms and handed it back. His existentialist side refused to cast blame elsewhere.

"Yeah, unfortunately." Stacy filed the forms away. "If I could give you some advice?" She asked rhetorically. "I'd recommend not giving her any reasons to fire you. She's been looking for one."

"You're right, but, according to the guys, it sounds like she doesn't even need one." Referring to Phil with a look of gratitude, he pulled on his production smock.

"And, she wanted me to remind you to take your survey as well." She said with a farewell. Andrew gave a mischievous smirk. "Come on…don't be stupid. Remember what I said."

"Roger that!" The door shut behind him.

He went, before shift change, to the crows nest to get the plans for the night. Opening the door he saw Frank standing on the table making an ass out of himself for the amusement of the supervisors. A terrible squawking sound emanated from Frank's mouth. The showman in him surfaced yet again. *I know this place will drive you nuts but really? Have some dignity!* Frank liked to believe he was an actor, along with the theatre he had also been in a couple commercials here and there; most prominently an impotent man in a Viagra commercial. He used more bronzer than George Hamilton, and his hair and teeth were whiter as well. One would think it a mid-life crisis, but rumors had him acting this way going on four years, much too long for a brief crisis. No, this was just Frank.

"What the fuck?" Andrew said, particularly blasé, as the door shut behind him. Garnering everyone's attention for the moment. "Come on." He rolled his eyes and tried to skirt the situation. "Let's be a little professional."

"Didn't you get the email?" One of the supervisors said, yelling above the squawking. Andrew shrugged as the question hit his back. "Nevermind. Frank sent out an email. It was a picture of six seagulls standing in a pyramid, shitting all over the one's below them." Andrew shrugged again and gave an expression that indicated 'okay, I'll bite'. "It was called Seagull Management." Still trying to explain to Andrew, while all the others were holding their sides.

"Patty is a bird brain. She practices seagull management." Frank paused his antics to attempt an explanation. He jumped off the table, put an arm around Andrew, and told him to 'picture this', pointing to the sky. "She soars high above, too high to really see anything." He paused for dramatic effect. "But, then, suddenly she swoops down, stomping her feet, squawking loudly, and shits all over everyone." He said looking up at the ceiling tiles as if they were broadcasting a movie. "Can you picture it? - Then she flies off like nothing happened."

Andrew sat at his computer, trying to work, and overcome by the ruckus behind him. *They all fucking laugh likes it's some joke. Yet, no one says a damn word when it's actually happening. Nothing is gonna change if nothing ever changes. She ain't gonna wake up one day, have an epiphany. She's not gonna say, 'Hey, I've been a huge bitch', come to work and apologize, and then we all go off eating cotton fucking candy and ice cream, holding hands singing Kumbaya.* He logged into his email, skipped over some routine end-of-shift messages and the .pdf from Frank, and opened the one titled 'employee engagement survey invitation'. *Time for a change.* The words poured out easily, as his experiences at Drury clashed in direct opposition with what he was learning in school. He held back nothing, it was everything he wanted to say but never grew the nerve to. It was the pinnacle of passive aggressiveness. Proud of his work, he cracked his knuckles and reviewed his comments for issues with spelling, grammar, flow and consistency. *If this doesn't get their attention then nothing will. Send?* His mouse pointer hovered over the finalizing button.

"If you aren't laughing over the email then what the hell is with that ridiculous smirk?" Lindsay asked his young protégé, as Andrew basked in his own glory.

"Nothing. Just sowing the seeds of discord." He swiveled his smile to greet Lindsay and clicked the button, the SOS was sent.

"I don't get you sometimes. We know you're smart, you don't need to speak above us. English son!" Lindsay only said what everyone else thought one time or another.

"Just, trying to change things for the better Lindsay."

"What? Like incite a rebellion?" He joked.

"Yeah." He said with delusions of grandeur.

"You're an idiot. The best outcome you could hope for from this.." Lindsay tapped the computer screen with his yellow, cracked fingernails. "would be something along the lines of the French Revolution." Andrew gave him a blank stare, he obviously didn't understand. "Kill a king, get a tyrant."

"Whatever. I'm thinkin' more like the Scottish Rebellion. Like William Wallace."

"You *are* an idiot. I'm guessing you watched Braveheart lately." Lindsay said with a huff and a puff. "Did you finish the movie?"

"No, power went out. Why?"

"Figures. You know, for someone so business savvy and smart you really need to brush up on your history. Anyway, you worry too much. Don't be so damn serious, laugh a little, and let that shit go! Now? If we're all done with the history lesson can we get some work done?"

13

Retirement

[I Got Friends in Low Places- Garth Brooks]

It smelled like stale sweat, flat beer and cheap cigarettes, making it impossible to breathe without it swirling around the sinuses. Neon Premium, Leinenkugel and Old Milwaukee signs flickered between the Big Buck Hunter machine and a wall full stray darts. Every beer mug was topped off with roughly three inches of thick foam.

The American Legion was only fitting for a few celebratory events, Lindsay's retirement happened to be one of them. The bartenders, waitresses, even the dishwasher all knew Lindsay, apparently it didn't matter that the legion was a half hour deep into Wisconsin. The bar manager must have figured the public smoking ban didn't apply to his establishment, as nearly every table had an ash tray, and nearly every ash tray had at least six cigarettes in it. The turnout was great, everyone from work was there; all the supervisors, Hollywood, Char, virtually all the staff members that had the night off, the only one missing was, of course, Patty.

"So, what's next hun?" A heavy-set, big breasted female in a partially torn Lynard Skynard T-Shirt asked from behind the bar, pulling her long greasy hair back from the far-from-clean glassware. Apparently no one had informed her of the wispy, almost translucent stray hairs that inched out from her chin and above her lip.

"Just go with the flow, I guess." Lindsay said. "I got no plans." Enjoying yet another beer on the house.

"Go get yourself a nice one-kicker and come ride with us." She slid him a blue bandana; an open invitation to join the club.

"Might take you up on that. Pension takes a couple months to kick in though." Lindsay rubbed his mustache in thought. "Hey kid." He twisted in his stool toward Andrew. "I got ya somethin'. Kind of a going away present."

"You're the one retiring." Andrew reminded him, sticking his finger in the foam hoping to kill it.

"It's out in the truck, come on." He patted Andrew on the knee like a grandfather to grandson. Deep in hardwood hunting country it wasn't uncommon for patrons to step out of the bar with their beer in hand. "So, I figure you'll need this more than I will now." The retiree pulled the shotgun from the wooden rack fixed to the back of the cab.

"Thanks." Andrew said as Lindsay placed his beer in the truck bed then handed Andrew the twelve gauge.

"Feel free to stop on by anytime if you need a place to let loose."

"Oh, I will. I'll bring a Gaylord full of watermelons too." Andrew said while holding the slug thrower in his hands.

"I can trust you won't go do nothin' stupid right." Lindsay wiped the foam from his mustache. "It's still registered to me."

"Yeah, no problem. Thanks again." Andrew said admiring the gun while walking it over to the Saturn. "It's still fine if I crash on your couch tonight right?" He was rudely reminded of the driving constraints after he opened the back door.

"Yeah, not a problem. Remember where the toilet is though, that couch has enough piss stains." Lindsay laughed, and followed it up with a big chug of beer.

The two odd friends headed back into the bar, Andrew patting his old pal on the back in appreciation. Upon their return, on the bar, in front of Lindsays stool, were a stack of presents and cards.

"Congrats Lindsay!" The crowd yelled, mostly in unison.

"Thanks everyone. Thank you." Lindsay attempted to shirk being the center of attention. He began unwrapping the gifts at the behest of the group. The cards all said the same thing, the gifts almost all gift cards, with a few exceptions.

"You gotta play it loud, man, LOUD. It's the only way." Hollywood said fixing his frizzy man-perm. Lindsay unwrapped the home-made Magnavox mix tape, quietly reading the hand written track list, either not knowing or hating every song. *Who has a tape player anyway?*

"I gotta take a leak." Andrew told the 'man of the hour', who nodded in acknowledgment. He put his mug down, and staggered his way off to the ill-kempt, closet of a bathroom.

"Thanks Hollywood." Lindsay was appreciative. It was the thought that counted; and for someone that hadn't been there long, he cared enough to get him a gift. He sat and unwrapped present after present, thanking each person in turn.

"Oh, sorry man. Damn, this thing is tiny." Hollywood said as his big hair entered first into the one toilet, one urinal bathroom. "Time to party." He finagled a dollar bill out of his tight, bleached and ripped jeans, then rolled it into a tight straw. "You party?" Andrew shook his head. "Well?" He sat on the toilet lid and drew up two lines of cocaine on a compact mirror, which apparently served two purposes.

"Fuck it." Andrew said as he shook off the piss and zipped up.

"Yeah man. Fuckin'-A right man." The perm bounced as he showed his enthusiasm with a shaka sign. He looked up to his supervisor, his eye liner a little blotched from sweat, and handed him the damp but crusty bill. "YEAH! Party time!" He said as Andrew snorted the white powder. His nostrils arid, dried out. He shuddered as it invaded his sinuses, stinging at first then nothing. "Take a gummer." He demonstrated for Andrew, licking his finger, covering it in the powder, and rubbing it against his gums. "Ah, yeah. All night long my man." The cocaine tasted bitter, his lips curled as his gums soaked up the drug. A sudden surge of energy took Andrew over, he hurried back to his mug, the staggering gone.

"Looks good, what is it?" Lindsay queasily regarded the grey, fleshy, oily ingredients in the Tupperware container, and asked the nice but incredibly intoxicated, homely baker.

"It's a secret recipe. A favorite of my neighbors in the trailer park, and my dogs." Char leaned in toward Lindsay, cuffed her mouth, and covertly whispered.

"Ahh. A secret." Lindsay winked, then smiled at his drunk friend. "Can't wait to try it." He didn't want to try it.

She couldn't keep the secret, she desperately wanted him, and everyone to like it and her. The alcohol severely hindered her patience, and vanquished her inhabitations.

"It's squirrel chow mein." She said with a prideful smile, baring more gums than teeth.

"Squirrel?" An astonished Lindsay asked for clarification. "Really?"

"Yes, silly." A drunken giggle snuck through her rotting teeth, seeing nothing peculiar about her gift.

The party raged on with darts and billiards and dirty mugs of foam and beer. Some danced to songs when Hollywood wasn't pumping the jukebox full of hair band crap. Some sat at the bar, chewing the fat, discussing anything other than work. Last call was less than an hour away, and the local crowd thinned out. It was more or less a Drury Lane party now. Lindsay kept his seat warm, not having moved since he and Andrew returned from the truck.

"Uhhhh." Frank slurred, drunkenly dropped a hand on Andrews shoulder, then slammed his beer on the counter.

"What is it man?" Andrew asked, mildly on edge from the combination of the cocaine and Franks sloppiness.

"Uhhhh. Check it out." Frank sloshed his beer around as he tried to point with the mug. "Party's over."

"Lindsay, Lindsay. Congrats, sorry I'm late." A blistering wind burst slid in through the side door with her, almost unnoticed. "Bet you never want to see another muffin again." She attempted the type of small talk which came normal to most.

"Yeah, but I couldn't go a day without seeing a donut though." Lindsay rattled back to her, they both laughed. The bar was still busy enough that she hadn't noticed Andrew. Festivities continued but age and the effects of alcohol kept Lindsay from staying until close. With a few kind words to the people around him, Lindsay rounded up all the gifts and moseyed over toward Andrew.

"You ready?"

"I'm not tired but sure." Andrew obliged his ride. "Was that Patty?"

"Yeah, nice of her to show."

"Uhh. *Surrrre* old man. Has she fleeced you too?" Andrew

chuckled, looking across the bar at his nemesis. Lindsay didn't respond, just gave him a headshake accompanied by a sly grin.

"Sometimes a nice gesture, can be just that. A nice gesture." He shared a pearl of wisdom from years. A little worse-for-wear the old man pulled his plaid flannel jacket on, tapped out a cigarette, and handed Andrew the gifts. "You're too young to be so cynical. That's for old people...like me." He laughed and lit up the cigarette. The red Chevy was just like its owner: old and reliable. It started up without incident. Lindsay went out to scrape the ice off the windshield.

"What is this stuff? Looks terrible-Smells worse." Andrew leaned out the window, holding up the Tupperware container.

"Gift from Char. Squirrel chow mein." Lindsay said, watching all the color disappear from Andrews face as his head jerked back in disgust.

"Squirrel?"

"That's what she said." The cigarette let out puff after puff, as he chiseled away at the ice.

"You aren't planning on eatin' it are you?"

"I think not. But, I wasn't about to insult someone after giving me a homemade gift." He said re-entering the cab.

The parking lot was a mess, it hadn't been plowed in days and there were no clear parking spots. Lindsay palmed the gearstick and dropped it into low, managing the beer and road conditions was going to take some finesse.

"Wait." Andrew said excitedly as a half-baked idea hammered at his skull. Lindsay feathered the clutch to keep it from dying. "Might as well make use of it right?" Andrew laughed and jumped down from the truck with the Tupperware.

"Come on, let's go, it's late." He honked the horn. Andrew made a bee line for the severely out-of-place and impeccably clean SUV. Stealthily, he opened the back door and slid the package in, then sprinted back unnoticed to the truck, gleefully laughing like a teenager. "What was that about?"

"Re-purposing the gift!" He rubbed his cold hands together, warming them with a long exhale.

"Calm down kid. Jesus, are you sweating?" He asked his oddly behaving friend, then pulled a joint from his jacket. "Anyways, this'll take the edge off... So, you still going to that shrink?"

"Yeah, same toilet, different shit. He put me on some new meds but it ain't workin'. Still getting headaches every morning." Andrew said and pinched the joint.

"Well, stick it out kid. I mean, it ain't like they just give out PhDs...And, the family?" Lindsay asked.

"Can't do it."

"What'd ya mean you can't do it. Family is the first and last thing ya got. Shit, I'd give my left nut for a family." The wayward veteran said adjusting his crotch. "Well, if Charlie didn't go shoot it off. Anyway. Don't get lost in all this shit man, it's a slippery slope. Remember what really matters, call her!"

"Alright, Jesus. But, she doesn't understand. I've told her I gotta leave this toxic place, quit this job, start over with my degree. Ya know? But, she says we can't afford it. I keep telling her I'm losing my shit. And, I *am* losing my shit! I swear I'm gonna crack one of these days." Andrew felt relief, able to finally get it off his chest.

"No problem is so big you gotta give up your family, figure it out kid." They passed around the joint for a few, long minutes. The windshield wipers had difficulty keeping up with the snow. "W. W. W. D." Lindsay said, seemingly snatching random letters from the air.

"What? Are you high?"

"What Would Willie Do?" The aged cowboy said inhaling the sweet smoke. "I tell ya what he'd do. He'd smoke this joint and pick his guitar, singing in the finest southern drawl, about how you gotta grow a pair." He coughed, laughing at his own joke. "Shit…That's what Willie'd do."

"You're too much man." Andrew thought his friend was a little spacey.

"Just sayin' young buck. She ain't gonna wait forever for you to figure it out. Remember, she's got *your* kids to think about too."

"You wanna be my psychologist?" He said wiping the perspiration from his face with an already sweaty palm.

"Screw you kid. Don't piss on my couch." He joked as the red Chevy pulled onto the gravel road that led to his trailer.

14

Awards

"Good morning, Drury Lane Bakery- Woodbury, this is Stacy, how may I help you today?" Her warm greeting, although standard for all callers, was still welcoming, even ones with an area code as strange as this one.

"Ahhh, si. Scusa miss." A man said in a thick Italian accent. "I hem docktore Moretti. Possibile speaka to a Patty Drury?"

"May I ask what this is in regards to?" Stacy questioned.

"Her figlia—scusa—daughter. Missa Grace Polita." The doctor cleared his throat. "There was an incidente."

"Oh, yes. Let me get her for you." Stacy responded with concern and placed the man on hold. Stacy sped down the hallway, and attempted to collect herself outside Patty's office.

"Come in." Patty said, sensing her presence on other side of the door.

"Yes, Patty…" Stacy said, while noticing Patty looking into her pocket mirror, powdering her face. "There is a man, sounds Italian, says he's a doctor and that there is a problem with your daughter." Stacy spat out. "He's on line one."

"Thank you, thank you." Patty said with appreciation as she shooed Stacy out the door and picked up the phone in one motion. "Hello, this is Patty."

"Ahhh, si, Missa Patty. I hem docktore Moretti. Your daughter hasa been in a incidente." The doctor spoke in broken English but the stressful concern was still apparent.

"Is she okay?" Patty asked.

"Ahh. Scusa." The doctor pardoned himself. There was a little ruffle through the phone.

"Hello, Patty? I'm a visiting student doctor here at the hospital. I hope you don't mind, doctor Moretti's English isn't the greatest. With regards to your daughter, she is conscious and okay, but she cannot speak or move much. She was in a Smart Car accident, and has suffered many broken bones and a crushed larynx." The young attending doctor said.

"Grace. " She whispered to herself. "Oh my goodness. How is Richard?" Patty asked about her daughter's new husband.

"Uh, I'm afraid I don't know how best to say it….I'm sorry miss, but Richard did not make it. Their Smart Car was hit on the drivers side while crossing an intersection." She gave Patty a moment. "Would you happen to have his families contact information?"

"Ahh, yes." Patty said fraught with unusual emotion. The conversation continued for many more minutes. Patty's worry would be visible to anyone, if they were in the room. As the conversation ended, Stacy saw the red light go out on line one.

"Is everything alright Patty?" Stacy asked from the doorway. "If you need anything please let me know."

"I'll be alright Stacy. Thanks for your concern." Patty said quietly. "What time is the car coming?"

"They are scheduled to pick you up around five pm." Stacy responded, a furrow of confusion crossed her forehead. "Why? Do you want me to cancel it? I'm sure it's not too late."

"No, don't worry about that. Could you try to find me a flight to Venice? Friday after work or the weekend would be fine." Patty said.

"Are you sure you don't want to find one now?"

"No, I said it's fine. Now, if you don't mind." Patty said referring to the time, and the makeup she still had to put on.

"Sure." Stacy left without issue. *What a psychopath, mother of the year.* An hour or so passed before Stacy would see her again, this time, Patty's make-up was complete. A porcelain doll in a charcoal pants suit with matching heels, she had tamed her once frizzy black hair, all she needed was a black veil and the look would be complete. Bright red lipstick, a golden wristwatch, and a slight pink hue of blush the only hints of color. The clock in the lobby read four-fifty-five.

"It's here." Stacy informed Patty.

"Thank you. Remember to find a flight." Patty directed her, while pulling on her petticoat, scarf and gloves; all black.

The elegant, hearse colored Lincoln Town Car was only partially visible through the storm. A driver emerged, holding the back door open. Patty stepped in, disappearing behind the dark tinted windows. The ride from Woodbury to the Walker Art Center wasn't long, but the snow and rush hour might affect it. St. Paul was the headquarters for the third generation, multi-million dollar company. Peter had rented out the large theater to host the annual meeting, it would be a full house with all fifty plant managers, thirty logistics managers, fourteen bakery outlet managers, six regional directors, and the entire corporate headquarters all in attendance. It was a celebration of self, a golden lesson in hubris.

Many people waited outside the building in the snow to get a quick cigarette in. They all took pause as the Town Car pulled up and the driver circled the car. They were curious as to who was so important, rumoring amongst themselves between puffs. The rumors would become nastier once the old widow exited the vehicle. Amongst those in attendance, the overall attitude toward Patty was almost equally split between animosity, intimidation, and a bothersome irritation. Of course there were still a few outliers, naïve newer managers that felt a misplaced pity for her.

"Good evening Patty, welcome." Rita, the human resource director, greeted Patty as she entered the building. "And, congrats."

"Thank you. We worked pretty hard to lower that CPU."

"Well, great job, enjoy the evening. There are beverages available in the lobby, and when you're ready, you can find a spot in the theater. The meeting will start in about twenty minutes."

"Thanks." Patty said and headed toward the lobby.

Contemporary, abstract art hung from every wall. Each with a story only the creator truly knew. Even the vibrant colored artwork couldn't warm up the cold, clean stainless steel industrial environment. The groups and cliques which huddled together, blowing steam from coffee, turned simultaneously to watch the widow. Patty didn't care. *Jealous assholes.* She approached the bow-tied bartender with a nose ring, punk hair and hipster ear piercings. She couldn't understand the fashion or the reason it was becoming acceptable in the corporate world.

"What would you like Miss? Cappuccino? Latte? Perrier? San Pelligrino?" His assumptions were wrong.

"Vodka, on the rocks, or neat. I don't care." Patty said. The young man bent down to grab a bottle. "No. Top shelf." She corrected him.

"The open bar tab is for rail only." He corrected her.

"Top shelf, rocks or neat. I'm not going to argue with you." She said unflinching, looking him straight in the eyes. She would happily argue all day, but the veiled threat was sufficient.

"Top shelf, neat." He repeated back, nodded and placed an embroidered napkin down then sat a crystal clear Old Fashioned glass on top.

[What I Am- Edie Brickell]

"Thanks." She winked and methodically twisted the glass clockwise with her fingers. While sipping, Patty perused the art collection and the collection of people. A squint, a leer, a snarl; the room was full of people who preferred Patty somewhere else. Even a pastel peacock displayed its beautiful pride, full of staring eyes that never closed. Another wall covered in ultra-feminine art; one, a hectic collage with a rough womanly figure that stood triumphantly in front of an unruly, non-descript crowd; another, a purposefully blurred picture of a bra in flames with the words 'do we hate our women?' frantically scribbled in permanent marker. She scoffed inside, she didn't understand any of it. The more she looked at the people and the art, the more they all looked the same. They just disappeared into the background. She finished the last sip of vodka and tapped the Old Fashion glass on the bar.

"Another?" The hipster asked.

"Indeed." She said, trying the aristocratic response with blatant sarcasm.

"Please find a seat in the auditorium. Peter will begin speaking in five minutes." The HR director spoke above the crowd, repeating herself in multiple locations.

"Make it a double, and make it quick." She told the young

man in response to the announcement. She grabbed the glass, emptying it with bigger, longer sips. More eyes, more of the crowd watched. Finishing the glass, she filed into the queue. Rubbing elbows with a bunch of young up n' comers; mostly men,with a few gorgeous women... *Hmm, wonder why you were hired?* Only a few seasoned managers remained, they were dislocated and 'on the outs'. Those around her smiled, or at least attempted to. Her cynicism wasn't far off from the truth.

She took a spot close to the back of the theater, knowing she would be accepting an award, this would give her more time to soak in the applause; however forced it was. The lights in the auditorium dimmed and dramatic, grandiose music gradually grew louder. As the crescendo hit an apex, two spot lights landed mid-stage illuminating a giant stylish, modern-looking logo; a monstrous, monolithic black steel outline of a muffin with clean, black initials DLB inside.

"Ladies and Gentlemen. Welcome." Peter strode in from off stage, a microphone on the lapel of his designer suit. "Welcome." He waved for the applause to come to an end. "Thank you, thank you."

"I'm sure we've all met before. But, I'm Peter Drury, CEO of this wonderful enterprise." He paused and pointed to the logo. "The Muffin Man is gone, but I still happily and humbly carry on his legacy. Welcome to DLB, the new Drury Lane Bakeries." He finished to a boom of applause and sounds of surprise and amazement. Peter spoke at length about the new company, and how it would surpass his fathers expectations. After the congratulatory remarks, the speech turned to the future of the industry and the companies competitive strategy, which was laid out by an expensive braintrust. Peter coveted the top spot in the industry, and would readily sell his soul to achieve it. Or take souls, whichever was required.

"Now, what many of you have come for." Peter announced, recruiting help from the CFO, CIO, and VPs who rose from their front row seats and joined him on stage. Larkin entered from the side and rolled out a decorative table which held laser-etched crystal trophies. Peter went on and on, gushing, detailing his pride in all the great work his team had accomplished. The ceremony began with the less acclaimed trophies in areas like 'best cakes' and 'best quality', eventually culminating in the top three trophies: Sales, CI, and Cost Per Unit.

"Sales, sales, sales. Our favorite word." Peter introduced the first big category. "No surprise here. Our winner again, year after year. Klayton and the team out in Denver!"

Klayton longed to be like Peter. He was a young, eager-to-please, kiss-ass, dressed in a finer off-the-rack suit and a watch that looked the part. This award was his retail locations third in as many years. Larkin stood shoulder-to-shoulder with Peter, silently presenting the awards as Peter congratulated each winner. After Klayton accepted the award and the roar from the audience quelled, it was time for the final awards.

"Here they are. CI and Cost Per Unit, the two most prestigious and coveted trophies." Peter panned a hand toward Larking who displayed the top awards. "Two trophies, one winner. Back on top this year. Please give a round of applause for Patty and the Woodbury team." The crowd stood, as was tradition, for the final awards. Patty let it soak in as the people around her patted her back and gave her a thumbs up. "Come on down Patty." Patty forced a look of astonishment, then rose from her seat, finding her way out of the row and down the long aisle to the stage.

"Her team was able to cut the cost per unit by over a dollar, and only in *six months*. Wow!" Peter looked thrilled. "And, listen to this, Patty also had the highest response rate for the employee engagement survey." Peter continued while Patty held the trophies for a quick picture with the CEO and Larkin. Patty was overcome with emotion; pride, confidence, and happiness. She cradled both awards in the bend of her elbow in order to wipe tears of joy from her eyes.

"Thank you, thank you so much." Patty gushed, kissing the awards, leaving behind her ruby lipstick. *Maybe Peter is coming around.* She began to step away as he placed a hand on her shoulder.

"And." Peter used the word to pause her momentum. "And, she was *also* the plant manager with the *lowest* employee satisfaction score!" The huge room was full of faces frozen in shock and awe. Patty, herself, must have caught her own reflection in the awards as she couldn't move either. "Who says you can't put lipstick on a pig!" Peter joked with his hand still upon her shoulder. Just as it appeared the entire room would die from lack of oxygen they burst into a boisterous roar of laughter, releasing Patty from her stasis. "Give her a hand ladies and gentleman, the manager one warmly referred to in the survey as the Machiavellian Mega Bitch, Ms. Patty Claron." He said with a final knife in the back. Then he covered the microphone on his lapel and leaned toward Patty and whispered, "you may go now."

15

Flooding

Technically it was spring, but in Minnesota, that only meant more sleet and less snow. It accumulated in wheel wells and around the soles of ones shoes. The parking lot was covered in thick murky grey sludge which turned to large black puddles when the sun decided to visit. Cars were everywhere, without order, due to the inability to see the lines. She stubbornly trapesed through the sludge in the black heels, leaving the hemming of her pant suit wet and sticky. An overworked umbrella kept her hair and the two crystal trophies pinned against her chest safe from the weather.

"Hello Stacy, any messages?" Patty asked in her nicest voice possible, while she shook the sleet from her umbrella and placed the trophies on the front desk.

"Nothing new. But, I got you a flight for Friday night, first class of course." Stacy said hoping to please her boss. "Looks like the meeting went well."

"Uh- yeah. You can cancel those tickets. I've got to take care of something important."

"Are you sure? Can I help you with anything?" Stacy offered, but thought 'what could possibly be more important than your daughter'.

"Yes. You can print off the employee engagement surveys for me." Patty said as she grabbed the trophies and left the wet umbrella on the desk. She made her way to the office, closing the door behind her.

Production was in full swing, the plant was a mess with busy bakers; with much more work needed than time available. Forklifts, pallet jacks, flatbeds, and cooling racks, which once moved with precision, began to deviate from their courses with reckless speed. Too much for too few, stress was amplified.

"Where do you need it?" Frank asked from the forklift as he pulled down a pallet full of cupcake packages from the top rack.

"Put it in the staging area by the cake room." Art said, his thumbs tugging on his belt loops. "Thanks."

Frank flew down the forklift lane, keeping the painted yellow lines on either side. Steam from the muffin pan washer flooded out from the sanitation room, making the concrete floors slick, but Frank was able to manage.

"Here is fine. We got a million orders of Easter cupcakes." Andrew said, hunched over a garbage can outside the cake room, waiting for the aspirin to kick in and take the edge off his hangover. "Uh, you drive through a puddle or something?"

"Sanitation." Frank mumbled, relaxing with a hand above his head grabbing the forklift cage. "Steam from the washer."

"Looks like more than steam." Andrew started off, and followed the wet tracks through the plant back to their origin. Frank followed him in the forklift, past the ovens and the sanitation room with the washer. "See." Andrew pointed at a huge growing black puddle which snuck under the emergency exit door and pushed toward the production floor. "Grab some wet floor signs, I'll let Patty know."

The building was old and poorly constructed. Whether it was a design flaw or faulty construction, the sidewalk outside the emergency exit sloped toward the building, causing puddles almost every spring. The worse the rain, the larger the flooding. Andrew double timed it back to the offices, knowing how fast the situation could escalate. With a hand on the door frame he hesitantly peeked his head past the threshold.

"Patty." She looked up from the papers, removing her Foster Grant readers.

"Yes, Andrew." She said in a reasonable tone.

"It's spring again. Water is coming under that emergency exit door." He reminded her of the reoccurring issue respectfully.

"Do what we did last year. Use a squeegee and place that rubber gasket that maintenance made under the door." She picked up her glasses, putting them back on her face and returned to the papers.

"It's pretty bad though. Is there any reason we haven't had it fixed yet? It's a safety hazard, and that gasket doesn't do much." Andrew carefully posed the question, trying to avoid pinning the blame on her, although he wanted to. Her index finger continued left to right, top to bottom, page to page. She was transfixed and obsessed with finding the culprit, completely ignoring the query. His patience diminished as she avoided answering him. He silently waited in the doorway for a forever minute, begging for a reasonable response, but none came. "Alright then." Her obvious lack of concern pestered him, to the point that his insides boiled with rage. He stomped off, the hangover taking a backseat, as he could hardly contain his ire.

[House of the Rising Sun- Animals]

"You okay?" Stacy asked Andrew, but nagging thoughts kept

him from hearing her, he passed her without a word or even a flash of eye contact. His consciousness swirled around and down his brain stem like dirty water in a toilet bowl, he was gone. Andrew's steel toed boots, which seemed to have gotten heavier, splashed black water around. The puddle had grown, now spreading out to about a hundred feet from the door.

"She having someone come out?" Frank asked, leaning on a squeegee. "This is a joke." He looked toward Andrew, who continued to stare down at the expanding blackness. "Hey, you, Andrew. You alright?" Again, Andrew wasn't able to pull himself together to join reality. The black, placid water swallowed all the color from his world, its encompassing darkness dominated Andrew; the abyss stared back.

"No. You think Art still has that OSHA ladies number?" Andrew kicked the water, which sent circular waves out in every direction. Frank said something but it didn't register with his brain. He splashed his way down to where Art was last. "Art…Hey, Art." He yelled down to Art as the fat man headed up the stairs. "You got that OSHA ladies phone number?"

"Yeah, probably in my email, why?" The stout supervisor was barely able to turn to Andrew as he took up the whole stair case, his gut brushing against the rail.

"I just need it."

"Alright, I'm heading up there right now. I'll get it for ya." Art could guess what this was about, but wouldn't recommend he do it, that is, if Andrew cared enough to ask his opinion. *It's your funeral buddy.*

"Son of a bitch!" She shouted while her fingers paced back and forth over the comment section of the surveys. The entire survey was available to all the plant managers, and it was a corporate recommendation to share the results and comments with the whole team. Most comments were short, vague, incoherent grumblings. This wasn't that, it was well written. It was a proclamation. It was a manifesto. Proper punctuation, proper grammar and large intellectual words. This was the work of someone with schooling, which severely limited the field.

"Should have figured it'd be you." Her fingers nearly scratching the paper from tracing the words for minutes. She moved from the paper to the handle of her desk. Without losing focus on the words, her fingers sprawled through the drawer until they touched the familiar curves. She twisted the perforated top, the cracking sound caused a conditioned physical response. Whetting her hostility, she sipped on the clear spirits, while re-reading the comments in her head.

How could Drury Lane Bakeries improve the employee experience?

Replace the plant manager. She is callous, uncaring and unethical. By choosing to remodel her office and trophy case rather than make the necessary repairs to the ammonia piping, she jeopardized the lives of all of her employees. In fact, an employee lost her life and I was hospitalized due to her hubris and clear inability to make the right decision. She has manipulated or threatened staff into unethical situations all for her pursuit of accolades and a bonus. The term 'Conflict of Interests' does not come close to describing her behavior. She places her own interests far above her staffs or the company as a whole. She is completely unhinged and unapproachable; having subjugated almost every employee into unquestioning obedience. She is a Machiavellian Mega Bitch. We all deserve much better here in Woodbury.

[Wonderwall- Oasis]

"Today is gonna be the day." Andrew said to Troy as he hung up the phone.

"I don't think you should've done that, she's gonna be pissed." Troy fretted.

"Yeah, don't you think you're making a mountain out of a molehill. I mean it's just some water, you're going a little overboard bud." Art chimed in, feeling it was time to talk some sense.

"Sh-sh-She said the last time-" Troy stammered, trying to warn him in a frantic but friendly tone.

"Am I the only one with a *fucking* spine around here? I don't care, it's done." An angered Andrew spun around in his chair to continue his work. They all punched away at their keyboards, adjusting schedules, completing forms, and filling out formulas. The unfinished issue still lingered about in the crows nest.

"Listen, none of us like her." Troy told him, with Art and the other supervisors nodding in agreement. "None of us. But, we all need this job." Troy still talking to Andrew's back. "I just hope you didn't get one of us fired." Andrew spun back around.

"I'm not afraid of that bitch. And, If I gotta be the one to take the heat so everyone else can be done with her, then so be it. Don't worry about your precious little jobs. I'll tell her to her face I did it myself." Andrew spun back around, his words and saliva flew into his friends face. He thought it was ridiculous, he was doing everyone a favor, and they wished he hadn't. *Cowards.* He rose from his chair, and descended the metal stairs. From the platform he could tell the puddle was still growing, it was now a good four inches deep, permeating at least half of production area. The dirty melted sleet splashed as the workers continued production regardless of the precarious conditions.

"Patty." Stacy said very quietly, peeking into the office, witnessing her drinking. "Ummm, Patty?"

"What? Don't you knock? What is it?" She didn't try to hide the bottle, she finished it, almost goading her to say something.

"It's important. Clara Foster called and said she was on her way here."

"What?!? Why?"

"Something about flooding."

"Son of a bitch." She tossed the bottle to the side and rushed out the office. "That son of a bitch." She repeated aloud and in her head as she hurriedly ran throughout the facility trying to find him. Her heels made a strange sound as they clicked through the dark, reflection-less water. He was now just ahead of her. "You're fired you little prick. Get the fuck out of here." She erupted as the production staff froze like ashen Pompeiian corpses. Andrew wondered if their silence stemmed from fear or if they suffered from Stockholm Syndrome; having been under her thumb for such a tenure.

"Don't worry I quit." He continued on his way out with her in tow.

"I know what you did, I know about all of it; my car, the survey, OSHA, all of it."

"Good." He kept walking, his feet trampling through the water. She kept after him, even following into the break room, berating him while others ate their lunch and watched 'Doctor Phil'. Andrew pretended like it didn't bother him as he grabbed his personal items and began out the door. He imagined doing an about face and raising her by the throat until the screaming stopped. Happily watching as the blood vessels shot like track marks across her eyes, her hands flailing, grasping at his fingers and the air she couldn't breath.

"Don't come back you little shit." She shouted from the doorway. He continued to his car. Opening the door, he felt a little safer, placing more distance between himself and his own machinations, and her. He tried to calm his nerves, inside he was a mess. Moments from peace, his eyes caught a glimpse of the breathalyzer which sent him spiraling out of control. He smashed it against the steering column until it broke into plastic shards which sliced his palms. A glint from an object in the rearview mirror only stoked his rage further; it was something he had nearly forgotten.

She was still advancing, unstopping, neither the weather nor Stacy standing in the doorway were able to hinder her progress.

"Get out here. I'm not done with you." She screamed, pointing to the spot on the ground at her toes, the cold sleet turned to steam as it hit her face. Her pace slowed but didn't stop when she saw it. The dark steel that laid in his hands was in deep contrast with his white smock. "What are you gonna do with that, you little pissant?" He stood motionless, his hands numb, feeling outside of his body. "You aren't gonna do anything. You're a coward like the rest of them. You'd be better off if you put that thing to your head and pulled the trigger." Still rooted to the concrete, he contemplated her words, unsure of his next action. "You can't win Andrew." Her hands strangling her small, black handbag.

"I know you Patty. I know you too well. Your overconfidence is your weakness." He broke his silence in a calm and collected manner. Placing the gun at his feet.

"Your faith in your friends is yours." Patty exclaimed in a quick, gritty retort. "Lindsay is gone and all the rest of them are sniveling peasants, happy I let them keep their crappy jobs. You aren't going to be a martyr Andrew. You're gonna be the next Phil." She said with spite, stepping forward further, the handbag she grasped fell into the slush exposing a tiny revolver in her hands. Her hands drew up, and Andrew continued to hold his ground. She inched closer until she was merely feet from him. "I'm doing you a favor." A spark exploded from the steel hammer, followed by a loud crack and a grey powder which lingered in the air. Then another spark, and another. Andrew fell to the ground holding his chest. She stooped over him as his chest jumped and his eyes gazed off into the overcast sky. Blood seeped from the holes in his white smock.

"Mmma—-mma—-maybe." He recruited the strength to spit out a few bloody syllables.

"Maybe what?" She asked as she leaned closer, admiring her deed.

"Maybe, you're...gonna be the one that saves me." Thick, clotting, crimson blood spilled out his mouth as it overflowed his lungs. His listless eyes angled, peering past her to the sky above, and a semblance of a smile drew across his face.

"Unlikely." She said snidely and spit a coup de grace at his feet.

16

Unevidenced

Yellow tape cordoned off the parking lot, workers and spectators watched the police as they scoured the area. The injured party was in the caring hands of the hospital staff and the shooter was detained, currently headed to the precinct to answer detectives questions.

"No shotgun sir." A clear skinned, clean cut young cadet addressed his senior officer.

"Wadding? Pellets? Cartridges? Anything?" The officer in charge asked.

"No, nothing. No slugs or shells either."

"Well, that doesn't add up. Did you search the whole lot?"

"Yes, the lot and all the vehicles. But-" The young man paused unsure if he should continue with his thought.

"Go ahead."

"But, there may be another victim, possibly a DB."

"What? What makes you think that?"

"The shooter's car...sir...it reeks of decomp...sir." His voice rattled excitedly, feeling like he cracked the case.

"Can you pinpoint the source?"

"No, sir. I don't think I can go back in there. I was choking down vomit the whole time."

"Gotta follow up on it rook. Perks of the job. Go put on some PPE if it bothers you that much." Suggesting the rookie go to the mobile crime scene trailer and put a mask and some protective gear on. About twenty minutes later they exited the trailer fully clad in white scrubs and bio-hazard respirators. The focus of the growing crowd beyond the tape shifted quickly to the shooters vehicle.

"She seems pretty normal to me."

"Those are usually the ones with the most to hide." The more experienced officer shared some advice from years on the job. "Just keep looking."

"What's this?" The rookie picked up a Tupperware container, the slimy grey contents sloshed around inside. "Oh my god. I'm gonna puke. —Is that brain fragments?" The respirators hardly made a dent in the stench, the rookie dropped the container and jumped out of the SUV.

"Let me see that." The other officer said, grabbing the container. "Idiot. That's squirrel chow mein." He brought the meal out of the car, displaying it to the nauseous rookie. "Where you from rook?" He quizzed the lad while placing the container in an evidence bag.

"Chicago."

"Well rook, welcome to Minnesota."

"Can you turn the heat up a little? It's cold back here and this plastic seat doesn't help." She said squirming around on the bench seat, with her face up toward the wire-mesh cage that separated front from back.

"Sit back please, Miss." The officer in the passenger seat said kindly, his body dwarfed by the back rest.

"Aren't you a little short to be a police officer?" The woman noir commented on his stature in a condescending tone. "How long is this going to take? I have an appointment with my psychiatrist at three."

"Probably not going to make that appointment." The older office driving the car looked at her in the rear view mirror. The squad car pulled into the underground prisoner drop-off, where she was released to two suited men. "Miss Drury, the Detectives will escort you now."

"I won't be sharing a room with anyone will I? They're all filthy. Germs." She swiveled her head side to side, shivering with disgust, and asked the detectives while walking past the holding cells.

"Just with us, for the time being." The men cordially held the door open for her, and asked her if she'd like anything to drink.

"Oh, how nice. Yes, coffee, but only if it's fresh, and single serve, and only if you have cream, regular cream, not that hazelnut foo-foo crap." The detectives looked taken aback.

"Okay. I'll be right back." One said as he removed the handcuffs. Leaving the two alone in the small, narrow room furnished only with two chairs and a table. Patty and the detective talked for minutes, mostly about life and work, nothing of substance. She began shifting her weight in the chair.

"No need to be nervous miss, we just have some questions. Mostly just routine."

"Where is he with my coffee?" She said just as the other detective entered with her beverage. "Oh, thank god. Who's your supervisor? I need to let them know about the service here." Taking a sip from the Styrofoam cup, and immediately spitting it back in. "It's *fucking* cold, and there is no cream! Can

I go now?"

"Alright. We'll get to it then." The detective sitting down placated her long enough, and wasn't going to let her debase his partner or the shield. "So, you shot him in self-defense?"

"Yes, self-defense. He had a shotgun pointed at me." She explained clearly, hoping that would be the end of it.

"Well, there is a problem with that. There was no shotgun found…anywhere. And, there isn't even a gun registered to him."

"That's just not true. You're lying, I don't appreciate dishonesty."

"No, Patty. It's true. You shot him, unarmed. You stalked him, hunted him down. He was a problem, so you removed him." Any politeness in his previous words was completely expelled.

"Ridiculous. Look at the video. You won't fool me into some coerced confession."

"Already asked for video. Apparently you had the service cut. Sorry, but, you won't be talking your way out of this."

"Get me your supervisor." She said completely ruffled. Completely oblivious to the gravity of the situation.

"It doesn't work like that Patty. We ask questions, you answer. That's it." The older detective said. "Now, what brought you to the parking lot?"

"Like I told the officers earlier—I was making sure he left the premises. I fired him and he had to leave."

"So, you weren't berating him? You weren't angry? You were just following procedure. That's what you're saying, that's your story?" The younger detective chimed in. "Cuz, that's not what others have said."

"What? What *others*? They don't know anything. He hated me, he always challenged me. Of course I was angry, but I was still following procedure. Ask the *others*, they'll say he had a vendetta against me, they'll say he was overcome with hate, they'll say he was willing to do about anything." She pointed at the younger detective, her words as black and bitter as the coffee in her cup. "Ask them! Or, ask yourself. What's more likely; a manager with no history of violence shoots an unarmed employee; or a drunk, depressed, headcase loses his grip on reality after being fired and pulls a shotgun on the one who fired him?" She had a point, from the perspective she left the detectives with the conclusion was evident.

"We don't care about speculation or what's more likely, we care about the truth and the facts. Two things you avoid, pepper with bullshit, or attempt to bend in your favor." The older detective was done with the interview, tired of the charade. "Either you're trying to mess with us, or your perception of reality is really fucked. Basically, you're either manipulative or you're crazy."

"Thank you, I'll go with crazy. Now, get me my lawyer, his number is in my black hand bag, you know the one with the gun—I'm sure you have that." She said smartly, purposefully knocking over the coffee, then folding her arms in victory.

17

Second Chances

[Burning House- Cam]

"Oh my god, oh-oh my god!" Her voice trembled, ached with fret, and her hands shook as she dropped the phone. "Christopher!" The words became caught in her throat. "Get your brother and pack a bag of clothes, dad needs us." She said with one hand half covering her mouth and the other sitting on her pregnant belly.

Her mind was everywhere, she couldn't make sense of anything. Life and love were turbulent enough, and the news of Andrew's assault stole whatever solidity remained. Still recoiling from the shock, she attempted the journey to the hospital, the minivan struggling to grip the road. Christopher asked about his dad, but the boys were too young to understand the circumstances, so she didn't try to explain. Somehow she managed the weather conditions, traffic, and her panicked state well enough to reach the hospital.

"Come on boys. Dad needs us." She said, unbuckling them and grabbing the duffle bag full of a random assortment of clothes and toiletries. They hurried into the ER entrance, pushing their way through the slow automatic doors. She sat the boys down, whispered a few motherly words to them, then went to speak with the intake desk.

"He is being operated on currently. When surgery is finished we will have a room for him, at that time you can join him." The intake nurse said, following procedure.

"Can you tell me how he's doing?" She pleaded.

"The notes say that he has multiple GSWs to the chest and shoulder area. Currently..." The nurse paused, while her fingers scanned the computer screen. "Currently he is critical, after performing an extraction his shock index is well above 1.0 and he is tachycardic-hypotensive." The nurse looked up from the screen. Andrew's wife wavered between hysterical and baffled. "After surgery, it looks like he still has internal bleeding."

"Oh, uh, please tell me he's going to be alright." The nurse returned her question with a blank look of contemplation.

"They will be giving him a transfusion and have to find the source of the bleeding. Tell you what, why don't you bring your kids to room 216. You can wait there." She wanted to help the poor woman, and that was the best she could do.

The moon light inched its way to the door. Inside the room it was silent, in the hallway it was hectic, only three inches separated the two. The boys slept haphazardly on the pull-out couch while she stayed vigilant from the chair. However, the four styrofoam cups of lackluster hospital coffee weren't enough to fend off her pregnant body's need for rest. She woke to the sound of the door.

"Good morning. You must be Andrew's wife." The doctor said as two aids rolled in the transfer bed tethered to a machine that tracked his vitals.

"Oh. Andrew." She jumped from the chair, tipping over the

coffee cups, rushing to his side. "Oh, sweetie. I should've listened to you. I'm so sorry."

"Miss?" The doctor needed her full attention. "Miss, your husband suffered some severe injuries. During the surgery, his body went into shock. He's physically stable now, his vitals are good for just having surgery."

"Oh. Thank you, thank you." She grabbed the doctors hand, but he still had more to inform her about.

"Miss? The shock and lack of blood flow to the brain." She stood in tears, holding the doctors hand and her husbands hand. She was happy and worried. "Miss. He is comatose.—He is in a coma." He spoke softly and clearly, while looking into her eyes to ensure the message was received properly. She trembled, her hands shot out to the bed rail for stability.

"But, he's alright right?" She asked again.

"Technically yes, but, Miss. With comas, there is no timetable for recovery, and when…or if he does come out, it is impossible to tell what his mental state will be." The doctor needed her to understand. Hope was all that remained.

For days his wife and their sons sat by his side, caring for their helpless husband and father. They bathed him and clothed him, read him stories and whispered loving words in his ears. Every morning, before the children woke, she would brush his hair and lovingly sing their favorite Van Morisson song. [Crazy Love- Van Morisson] The doctors said that although he could not move or talk, he could hear. This she clung to. Talking to him in every possible moment. It was just the four of them for a little over a week, until one early weekend morning.

"Hello?" An older gentlemen knocked, and waited for a response.

"Come in."

"Hello. I'm Andrew's friend, Lindsay, from work." He entered in clean, pressed blue jeans, a long-sleeve buffalo plaid shirt rolled up to the elbows, and recently shined cowboy boots. His breast pocket holding a pack of cigarettes. In his left hand a duffle bag and the right a floral arrangement.

"Very nice to meet you Lindsay. Thank you for your thoughtfulness."

"How's he doing?" He bent over his friend, laying a hand on his chest.

"His body recovered well. He is," she fought back the tears, "he is in a coma though-I'm sorry, but have we met?"

"No, however, he spoke a lot about you and the boys. —I know things weren't the greatest when this all happened."

"No, no, they weren't. But, that doesn't matter now." She said holding her husbands hand, firmly committed.

"Ummm, I hope I didn't overstep. But, I stopped by the house and picked up some of his things. You know, in case he wakes up, it'd be nice if he had some things from the house."

"No, not a problem at all. Actually, very considerate of you."

"There is one thing I think you should take a look at though. When I went through his stuff, I found this." He pulled a worn notebook from the duffel bag. "He was really going through some hard times. I thought I knew, but it was a lot deeper and darker than I expected. One thing is certain though, he really loves you and the boys, even if he didn't always act like it. You should really look through it."

"Thank you. I will."

Days went by, still no movement, not even a bat of an eye lash. His wife and children were the yin to his yang; they were restless, unable to sit still due to nerves, eagerness, frustration, hunger, and sun deprivation. She was packing up the boys items so they could head back to their home, return to school and live normal little boy lives. The notebook Lindsay had left still lay atop a pile of Andrew's items on the floor. She decided to give it a look, flipping it over revealed a strange, dark and prophetic quip etched into the cover.

> *'I am less than nothing in nobody land/ I do nothing better than nobody can/ I am fodder for the widow of the muffin man'*

Her curiosity piqued, and her inner concerns raised. She carefully thumbed through the spiral notebook, finding much more of the same.

> *'Island*
> *How dare you scrutinize me/ Who the fuck are you/ How dare you threaten me/ Your malfeasance will cause a coup/ I fear nothing spewing from your reprehensible lips/ Tactless, conceited and vile/ With a cockeyed half-veiled smile/ Go back from where you came/ I fear you no more/ Live out your days on that desolate island you've stranded yourself on/ Abandoned/ I feel bad for you/ Whether it's empathy or pity/ It is a human emotion/ One your lifeless body hasn't felt in years/ A grudge is a load too heavy/ I will not let ill will corrupt us both/ Stay on your island'*

His writing portrayed a different Andrew than she had known. She looked over at her husband with new eyes and caressed his hair. His emotions and psychology bounced from page to page like a ping pong ball; back and forth, switching directions, spinning wildly with each hit of the paddle.

'Committed
I was so committed/ I needed to be committed/ Put me in
a padded room with windows tinted/ A one-way mirror
to be exhibited/ Put me on display/ the epitaph would
say/ Here was a man who was committed all too long to
something unworthy'

Was this about work or us, his family? Maybe he wasn't distancing himself from them, but keeping them safe from the fallout of his inevitable collapse. The notebook was filled. It was as if Jackson Pollock took up poetry. Paintbrush bristles caked in a myriad of emotions, flicked and flung, sending drops and dribbles of it this way and that.

'Where Does A Prayer Go?
Where does a prayer go/ Is it similar to a dream deferred/
Or does it sprout wings and leave this earth/ Past the
green canopy/ Past the cumulus clouds/ Past the orbit of
the ninth planet/ Or does it go deep, past the top soil and
granite/ Does it matter if it comes from me/ Or the sweet
songs of Amos Lee/ Does it flutter a few feet then fall/
Like a lonesome dove caught in a squall/ Or does it reach
the intended shores/ And who, if anyone, lends its course'

He was looking for answers. Looking for a way out. *Was he praying? That doesn't sound like him. He must be desperate for help.* She tried to picture when and where he wrote these poems. A cause, a reason, she tried to re-connect with her estranged husband.

Jealousy
*I watch with amazement/ Take in the beauty and the ease
in which you work/ How you handle all at once/ How
your love is constant, equal and complete/ With no valleys
or peaks/ Never rests and never sleeps/ I am jealous/
How you believe in the somehows and the somedays/ How
your faith always triumphs over certainty/ Grace under
fire/ I admire/ Your brilliance and an essence that never
tires/ I am jealous/ A model in both senses/ No fences/
Nothing can cage or bridal your fervor for life/ I watch
in amazement with curious delight'*

She was inundated with words and thoughts and feelings that she had never dealt with before. It was overwhelming, even the autonomous functions of the heart and lungs were effected. Her husband needed help. If he survived this, he needed some serious help, more than she could offer. It sounded as though he was lost, not feeling, or feeling too deeply. Detached from the reality that surrounded him, he was left adrift to battle the raging currents in his head.

18

Judgement

They gathered in a room of glossy, knotted, yellow pine and low-piled, grey commercial Berber carpet. The smell of fresh stain and carpet odor lingered from the previous days update. A cold steel, hard-wired clock over the bench kept the official time. Against the wall closest to the judges chambers stood an American flag and a state flag of Minnesota. They hung motionless, the fly end draped over the engraved state seal. A portly, elder bailiff strategically positioned himself between Patty and the judge, awaiting further instruction. Words echoed easily and endlessly throughout the empty gallery behind her.

"It is the opinion of this court that the defendant was, at the time of the offense, not of sound mind." The old man, drowning in his robe, cleared his throat then spoke, to the dismay of the prosecution. "Please." He said quietly, as the DA's table grumbled. "Let me explain."

Pattys shoulders slumped as the mounting tension in her upper body abruptly vanished. One of her well-dressed, six-figure lawyers placed a congratulatory arm around her, as she let out a sigh of relief, followed by an autonomous roll of her eyes. Prior to litigation, her lawyers advised her that a jury may not fully understand the intricacies of an affirmative defense, and that having a judge, especially this judge decide the case, would be the best course of action.

"In an affirmative defense case, such as this, the defense's sole responsibility is to simply prove that at the time of the crime the defendant either did not know the quality of their actions, or that if they did know, that they did not know they were wrong." The judge removed the circular frames that dangled from the tip of his red bulbous nose, and made sure his explanation was understood by the two younger judicial trainees that sat beside him. As the words finished bouncing from the back wall, he continued.

"The defense has made a solid case. Between the state psychologists opinion, the psychological and emotional damage from earlier domestic violence, the recent loss of her husband, the chronic alcohol abuse and the mounting pressures at work, they have been able to meet the requirements of the M'Naughten rule. Even the prosecutions character witnesses testimonies ended up strengthening the defenses case." He spoke directly and firmly. Age and alcohol did not effect his mental prowess. The gavel looked ready to fall.

"This does not mean I condone the egregious act, nor does it mean my sympathy for her will outweigh that of the real victim. I do believe the DAs office failed on this most important case." His tone changed dramatically, he spoke much more from the heart than the law books. "I am afraid we may have set a scary precedence here." His eyes moved away from the prosecution and froze firmly on Patty. The bailiff stepped closer to the tables of the defense, as the judge neared the end of his speech.

[Mean- Taylor Swift]

"Miss Drury, please stand." The judge asked calmly. Her lawyer patted her on the shoulder as she took the direction, a stealthy smile was eager to reveal itself. "Miss Patty Drury, you have been found not guilty by reason of temporary insanity. You are to be committed to the Northern Pines mental health facility in Brainerd until you are no longer deemed a threat to this community. - I-" The gavel dropped. Patty began fidgeting with her hands, words forced there way to her tongue, preparing to erupt until the lawyer closest to her grabbed her hands and slightly shook his head. "I certainly hope you are able to find some clarity Miss Drury. And, consider yourself lucky. If the trial had turned out differently; if the victim was well and willing to testify, you might have been sentenced to many years."

"Your honor?" The prosecution pleaded, "your honor?", only receiving the consecutive knocks of a gavel. "Please look again, re-evaluate her character, please." The district attorney begged the sinewy, twelve stepper.

"Mr. Ventura", the old man stared with perturbed eyes at the prosecution, while removing his microphone and robe. "If bad personality were a crime, the defendant would most definitely be imprisoned. However, here in the wonderful state of Minnesota bad personality is not a crime.—Bailiff, please escort Miss Drury to the processing area."

"Your honor, would you allow Miss Drury a chance to get her affairs in order before the committal?" Her astute young legal aide asked.

"Not a chance young man. Between posting bail and the length of this trial she has had more than enough time. Minnesota needs her to get well." Nothing more needed to be said. The judges exited toward the chamber room and the bailiff nestled up to Patty, taking her by the wrist.

She waited for her name to be called like every other common criminal, except that her bus would be going somewhere different. The hard plastic, indestructible, immovable seats were extremely uncomfortable, and were dominating her attention. *This is ridiculous.* Shifting in her seat to no avail. She analyzed the occupants of the room, which only disturbed her more. *Why am I here, amongst all these derelicts, these detestable people? Ick!*

"How long is this going to take?" She stood and barked at the closest officer in the room, while her heels tapped away.

"Sit down miss. They will get to you when they get to you." The man replied, leaving Patty taken aback. *Rude.*

Some tried to engage her in small talk while they waited, but she made it a point to make them feel so unwelcomed that they discontinued their banter. She felt dirty, confined and debased. *I'll be out in a week.* The thought was on a loop, coming around every ten minutes or so, for the entire three hours she sat in the hall.

"Patty Drury?" A woman announced from the safe side of a plexi-glass protected desk. Patty approached the glass. "Remove any personal items and place them here", referring to the slot in the glass. "Your full name, date of birth, social security and most recent residence." She probed with no pleasantries. Patty rattled them off, hoping that would be the end of the waiting. "Next of kin?" Patty shuddered, she had forgotten about her daughter and her ordeal. "Next of kin?" The lady repeated with a firmer tone. Patty's eyes welled up and her knees weakened, she felt on the verge of collapse. "Next of kin?" She demanded in frustration. "Guard!" She yelled and tapped on the glass, pointing at the old, weepy, feeble woman. "She's non-compliant and uncooperative. Take her to the bus." The guard forcibly grabbed her upper arm, dragging her to another waiting room, this time the room was full of fidgety, unblinking women who only looked at their feet, the wall, or into another dimension.

"Sit. Don't move, or I'll be forced to restrain you." His eyes spoke loud enough to make his tone irrelevant. This room had no clock, no pictures, nothing that wasn't fastened to the ground. It had to have been another hour, at the very minimum, before anyone entered the room.

"Role call. Line up at the door when you hear your name." A uniformed man said as he entered in from an external door. The women followed instructions until the all seats were empty. "Follow me, and file to the back. Take the first seat available." The seats on the bus were almost as intolerable as those in the first waiting area, she dreamed of her office chair. *Next of kin?* Her mind kept reverting back to it, and her body reacted the same as before.

She watched, with her head in her hands, as the sidewalks turned to farmland, and the maple trees to birch and evergreen. Terrible suspension made for a rough and loud ride. Daisies sprouted between dandelions and ditch flowers, reaching for the cloud covered sun. Rays flickered between the bars on the windows, casting horizontal shadows on the seat before her. The warmth of the rays and the quiet crowded benches had her drifting away from the squeaking suspension. A grinding sound paired with the bus physically shaking eventually ripped her from her day-dreaming. Ahead, past a row of pine trees and a tall fence, a drab, egg-shell white brick building appeared. No signs or colors, or any identifiable markings; it was sanitized for the outside world. Designed to bleed into the background, it was a place to ignore, a house for the undesirable, the unfit; a place to pretend never existed. *I'll be out in a week.* She thought, somewhat believing positive thinking would affect her length of stay.

"Welcome to Northern Pines." A friendly woman greeted them one by one as they entered. "How are we today Patty?"

"Ah, I've had better days. How long do you suppose I'll be here?" Patty asked.

"Don't worry about the length, just enjoy and appreciate the time. I'm sure after a couple days you wont be too concerned about it." She reassured here, and tried to calm the visibly unstable woman. "Heather, here, will help you get acquainted with the place, and show you to your new room. Once you're settled, we'll discuss your MMPI results and our care plan."

"Thank you." Patty said, still a little uneasy, untrusting and shaky. She disappeared down the long, wide, laminate floored hallway a step behind Heather.

19

Realization

[In the Waiting Line- Zero 7]

"Everyone's saying different things to me." Patty said, her words soaked with disdain. "There doesn't seem to be anyone else who agrees with me." Her face hot with emotion.

"Patty." The woman said calmly, hoping it would be contagious. "You shot someone, you do realize that don't you?"

"This is ridiculous, he had a gun pointed at me. No one believes me!" Patty fought back, still trying to justify her actions to them and to herself.

"Can you say it aloud?" The therapist asked. "I think you'll find it cathartic. Once, your able to admit it to yourself, then we can talk about how much longer you might be here." The therapist crossed her legs then straightened her dress pants. "Give it a try. Say, 'I shot him'." She challenged her. The room was silent for a few moments with only the clock noticeable.

"You're wasting my time." Patty parried and broke the silence with a jab.

"That's all you have now Patty. Time." The woman jogged her memory, keeping her abreast of the situation. Recognizing the brick wall before her, she turned to her desk and began typing on the computer. "I am placing you on a new regime of Risperdal and Nortriptyline. It'll help you deal with your emotions responsibly, we'll watch closely. Let me know of any side effects or concerns." She escorted Patty back down to her room. "Take care of yourself Patty."

"Wasting my time." The bitter old woman repeated again and again, as she paced back and forth in her insanely bland, cream colored, sterilized room. It'd been well over a month since she arrived, and her certainty of leaving was fading. *Wasting my time.* She kicked the wall, which did nothing but hurt her toes. *Next of kin?* She sat down on her bed. *Grace.* Her mind flooded with joyful motherhood moments: baths, highchairs, first words, counting her freckles, graduation, and taming her red hair. Then it whipped abruptly and distastefully without transition to Grace's father: belts, cruel words, fists, car doors, windows, booze. She began grumbling incoherently, "Wasting my time—time. Don't they know? He had a gun. I'm not, I'm crazy."

The grounds below her window sill changed uncountable times from green, to grey, to white, to murky black, to sandy, to grey, and back to green. She sat for endless hours watching from the bay windows in her room, with a new roommate every season, sometimes more often. The latest roommate was a twenty-something woman with red hair that was as frizzy and as crazy as her personality. She was pasty, pale and freckled, and attempted to sing along with every song that came over the speakers. Patty would have completely dissolved this ginger from her reality if it weren't for the uncanny resemblance to her daughter. Her name was Amber and she was bi-polar. Some days she would talk for hours, cheery and bubbly, while other days she wouldn't roll out of her bed for anything other than the restroom.

Today was an outside day, as suggested by the facility staff. A quarter of the courtyard was cast in shadows from the surrounding building, the rest was paradise. The bench they chose was still warm from the early morning rays. Patty closed her eyes after taking in the unobstructed sun. Negative images and bursts of color danced about, she slowly slipped into a daydream.

"Patty?" Her roommate pulled her from her trip.

"Yes Grace." Patty answered, an unnoticed Freudian slip, her eyes still closed and the images still dancing.

"Why don't you ever talk?" She asked, looking up at the sun with her arms raised to meet it. "I mean, I know I talk a lot. Like…a lot sometimes. But, you never talk. Never say more than like three words." Still looking at the sun.

"Nothing to say." Patty said her three words, while the images receded into the distance. "Why?" She opened her eyes and faced Amber as she explored the sky.

"I worry about you." The young woman said now placing a comforting hand on her roommates knee.

"*You?* Worry about *me?*" She snorted and removed the hand from her knee. "You have issues."

"You know, you're here too. They don't just keep a person here for a year or more if there ain't something wrong with 'em." She looked into her roommates eyes, searching for human emotion, there was none to be had. "If you ever want to get outta here, you might want to consider a little self examination."

"Says the woman that's been to three facilities in five years and has these." Patty grabbed Amber's wrists and turned them up, exposing numerous horizontal scars.

"All right. I'm done. I've sat in that bed for months, trying to have some sort of conversation. Trying to get to know you, trying to finally have a friend in here, but all you do is sit there completely emotionless like a fucking mannequin. That is until you decide to be a mega bitch and go off on everyone, even if they're trying to help you."

"Don't you EVER call me a mega bitch. You don't kn-"

"Listen, Patty, I'm not done. Yes, yes I have issues. Yes, that is obvious. I'm crazy, I'm not normal. I know that. But, I'm willing to admit it, and try to get better. While you—-you! You just sit there in your own little fucking world believing everyone else is wrong. At least I know when I'm hallucinating!" Her voice filled the courtyard, as if she was trying to speak from a mile away. Patty's eyes were the size of walnuts and her lips trembled. Amber was jumpy, on edge, now standing on the bench and flailing, attracting the attention of the facility staff. Patty saw her daughter behind the crazy façade. "Sometimes I wish I was hallucinating when I wake up to you every morning. I'm holding out hope for you Patty, but it's fading. I'm sure you've burnt every bridge, even the staff won't listen to you anymore, everyone's given up on you." She paused for a moment and grabbed Patty's hand, holding tight even while Patty fought to drawback. "You can't touch the world out there anymore, and even the crazy ass people in here can't reach you. That's why you never have roommates, no one can stand you. You're on an island, better swim to shore before you get too deep. Help yourself—-" The closest nurse came and attempted to restrain the red-head, but she required help. Patty sat stone-faced on the bench, now gazing at the sun, unmoved by the abhorrent scuffle. Her roommate was now on the ground, getting fitted with restraints. "And take your fucking medicine. I see you cheek it every time." She glared at Patty with crazed, vexing eyes and reached for her leg before she was finally restrained and a hysterical smile painted her face. "Kay?" She winked at Patty. The team of nurses fixed her to a wheelchair and removed her from Patty's life permanently.

Patty rested on the bench, looking up at the sun, disregarding everything entirely, and closed her eyes. Impossible imagery danced around without reason. Frizzy red fingers combed their way through the darkness.

"So—" The woman in the white smock said as she rearranged her desk. "In court that's called a mitigating circumstance, but here, in the real world—it's called an excuse." She wasn't going to listen to her about the shotgun any longer, whether it existed or not. "Listen, I don't give up on patients, I don't. But, I'm going to stop our sessions, they don't seem to help. Your delusions have you stuck, and I know you've been cheeking or refusing your medications. Either way, there doesn't seem to be much else I can do for you." The doctor admitted with displeasure and heartbreaking failure. With no roommates, and the nurses stopping medication, this was Patty's last connection to the world outside her head. Something deep and unknown prompted Patty to speak.

"What if—" Patty attempted.

"No, Patty. This is not transactional, this is not quid pro quo. This is and has always been your choice. If you've given up, then I must too. I will pray for you." The doctor looked on the verge of tears, she wavered on whether to leave the room, her voice welled up. "You know—" She debated on divulging personal information. "Your last roommate, Amber." Her hands shook uncontrollably. "She believed in you. She told me! She had a pure, youthful, unconditional love inside her, something you stole, something you haven't had since your late husband or daughter. And—" She began weeping, her quivering lips half-hidden between her slender fingers. "And after you gave up on your life, she took her own."

Patty wrestled with wild and unharnessed emotions that she had once seen in the movies. Although none surfaced, they raged without constraint inside. It was only a week later, as she sat in the courtyard that it consumed her. She placed a hand on the warm, empty spot of the bench, and spoke truth in whispers. The whispers evolved to tears which never ceased. She shut her eyes and looked to the sun, and the images danced about.

[Higher Love- Lilly Winwood]

20

Baggage

[Day of the Locusts- Bob Dylan]

An old box speaker teetered precariously above the ice freezer, it's thin paper cone peaked and popped with shrill music. The dust-laden oscillating fan that sat behind the service counter, offered little refuge from the heat which constantly pumped out of the vent at his feet. A number '2' light a few inches from his head, flickered in a headache-inducing, non-repeating sequence. It had remained that way for the past month, yet no one seemed to mind. One of the motors on the automatic doors had seized up a week ago as well, leading unfamiliar customers into the glass panes. These small, seemingly insignificant things used to nag at his consciousness and dominate entire days, now they were just trivial and only mattered for a minute.

"They back. Right around Thanksgiving every year." A mulleted, middle-aged man in a red vest, leaned over his register and tapped his co-worker on the shoulder. "Looks like they're makin' trouble already. Damn buck out here in Buffalo County attract all 'em." Pointing over towards the beer coolers, informing his new colleague of their seasonal clientele.

135

"Better go settle this. You know, it's a cardinal sin. Buck huntin' in an Escalade. Geesh, probably don't even eat what they kill. Probably just a set of antlers on their wall; trophies. Anyways, I gotta fix this. Damn." His animosity trailed off as he stepped away from the till and walked down the aisle, where there was a confrontation brewing between the customers and a young stock boy. Their loud voices carried throughout the wood-paneled corner store- something about not having some imported beer. The cooler doors slammed, and the arguing escalated. His downtrodden colleague carried himself and two cases of beer back to the front of the store. "Ring 'em up. I'll get 'em their chaw, it's on the house." He said, defeated and publicly humiliated.

"Afternoon gentlemen. Find everything alright?" The slender, amiable forty-something man asked while he scanned the items.

"You're fucking with me right? You didn't just—nevermind, just, how much do I o" Said a younger, stylish man in aviator glasses with a perfect five o'clock shadow, clad in Under Armor camouflage head-to-toe. His eyes drew up from the stack of fresh, sharp, consecutive hundreds in his wallet. "Andrew?" He asked, mid rant. The cashier looked up from bagging their beer, peanuts and beef jerky. "It's you isn't it? Christ, I thought you were dead. What the hell you doing out here in po-dunk-ville?"

"Well, I."

"Managing right? Not bad I guess. You finish your degree? A little over qualified for this shit I'd say." He spoke tartly, not the weak, submissive stammering Andrew remembered.

"Ye-"

"Gotta be a little difficult dealing with all these trained monkeys, seriously, if buck weren't everywhere out here, I wouldn't ever come out to this sorry ass place. Anyways, Christ." The man forgot about his friends. "Guys, this is Andrew. Remember that guy I told you about?" He looked away from the cashier and back to his comrades, pointing to his old friend. "Glad you're doing well. Better than Phil at least. You hear about him? Poor schmuck." He paused for a second, with no answer he continued on. "Still couldn't find work after five years, so he moved to Iowa or some shit for a fresh start, opened his own little used bike store-Pedal Phil's Bikes."

"That doesn't sound so bad." Andrew responded.

"It wasn't, until he hired a guy to do his signs. Phil was always cheap, you get what you pay for I guess. I mean, the sign was actually pretty nice minus one small thing. The word 'pedal', cleverly had a bike 'pedal' printed as the 'P', but the guy had 'Phil's' name in cursive and the damn 's' looked like an 'e'!"

Andrew mulled it over as he finished the transaction and handed him the receipt. Then it hit him. "Yeah, the fucking sign read Pedal Phile Bikes. It didn't help that the local commercials and billboards had kids hopping up n' down on the bike seat with a shit eating grin across their face, or the fact that he had been fired from his last job for sexual harassment. The small town turned on him quick. He packed that shit up and got the fuck outta Fort Dodge." Troy finished as his friends burst out in laughter, they'd heard all of Phil's follies countless times but they still loved them. Andrew just stood there, feeling sympathy for Phil, the man he never met but shared a lot of similarities. "Poor schmuck. —Jesus, I've been talking all this time. Christ, sorry, how are you?"

"Well, actually Troy, I'm great. Best I've felt my whole life. Working here part-time and being a full-time dad and husband. Feel like I'm finally hap-."

"Wait." The man laughed in disbelief. "You're a cashier?" He asked with a disrespectful chuckle.

"Yeah, so?"

"Wh-what d'ya make like nine dollars an hour? Don't you feel like a loser? Like you're unaccomplished? I mean shit, you're bagging my groceries for fuck sake." Throwing a mocking finger towards the red vest with a smirk.

"Well, Troy. I'm happy and I'm accomplished. And, this is a good place with good, down-to-earth people, a place where I don't have to check my integrity at the door, a place where my worth isn't calculated by my paycheck. I'm-." Andrew tried to explain.

"How can you say you're accomplished?" Troy asked, having blocked out everything Andrew had to say after that statement.

"Because, I've been able to raise three great kids and have a great marriage. How are you doing?" Andrew quickly replied then asked his old colleague, not feeling he had to justify his happiness any longer; ready to move from the subject.

"Oh, it's been great. After that whole fiasco between you and Patty, there was like a changing of the guard. A lot of positions opened up as the older managers '*left*'." He said making air quotes. "I got a promotion, then another one, then another one. Now, I'm Peter's right hand man-he fired Larkin, said he was 'talkin' to much', said he was becoming 'stale'."

Troy's crew headed out the door, hoping the conversation would end soon so they could get to drinking. While Troy, being as arrogant and self-aggrandizing as he was, couldn't pass up a chance to share the story of his success and wealth, even if he was mildly irritated only a moment before.

"Nice, congrats, you happy?"

"Of course I'm happy, why wouldn't I be?" Troy said, annoyed with the question, now eager to join his friends for beer and bucks. "Hold up. You aren't trying to do some Will Smith sentimental movie realization bullshit now. I mean you coulda been just like me, except you let your damn ethics get in the way of your ambition. You were a legend at Drury, even Peter heralded it as modern-day David versus Goliath. Shit, he even called you 'The Muffin Man'. And now! Now? Now, you're just a fucking loser bagging my groceries." Troy grabbed his beer and stomped away. Turning his head once, shaking it with disgust, only to be unexpectedly greeted by the faulty automatic door.

"Thank you. Have a good day."

21

Last Rites

The all black Audi sped down the narrow and wandering county roads, passing wayward farm animals, tractors, and broken down pick-ups. After blowing through the towns single stop-light, it cruised down the residential streets, rolling from block to block aimlessly. The drivers window rolled down occasionally, as a middle-aged man in sleek Bulgari sunglasses peaked out to examine the street signs. It gradually slowed to an idle in front a modest, stucco single story home in decent repair. The man exited the car; clad in designer jeans, patent leather loafers and a dark sport coat, and toting a manila envelope.

"Hello young man, is your father home?" He asked after removing his sunglasses and bending over to greet the young lad. The boy left the screen door closed and ran off without a word. A moment later returning with his father.

"Good afternoon sir. Are you Andrew?" He extended a hand while the father opened the screen door. "The Andrew that worked at Drury Lane Bakeries ten years ago or so?"

"Yes. What can we do for you?" Andrew asked, as the man shook his hand and formally introduced himself.

"I know it may seem a little odd, but I am here at the behest of a former client. You must have known her quite well, as this was her sole request." The man tucked his sunglasses in his breast pocket and presented Andrew with the envelope. "She wanted you to have this."

"Pardon me for asking, but who was your client?" Andrew asked with a little caution.

"A Miss Patty Drury." The man said clearly and without hesitation, oblivious to the history between her and the man before him. "She spoke very highly of you at the time we penned her will."

"Can I ask how she passed?"

"Certainly. Patty was, as I am sure you are aware, in the care of the staff at Northern Pines for the remainder of her life. This past week, she passed away there in Brainerd from congestive heart failure. The year before, she had a consultation with me and described what should happen if she were to pass. This-" He pointed to the envelope in Andrews hands. "Was her main concern."

"Do you know what's in it?" He asked the lawyer. "I mean it ain't like anthrax or anything right. Sorry, I don't mean to be cynical it's just-"

"No, no anthrax. Just something she wished you would read." The lawyer snickered then reassured him. "If there isn't anything else." He spoke respectfully and waited for a cue. "Then, I should be on my way. Enjoy the beautiful day." He turned to head toward the Audi, and finished with a few kind words about the area. "I didn't realize how calming it is out here in the country."

"It *is* a different way of life. Thank you." Andrew held up the envelope and waved.

The screen door smacked the frame loudly, its spring rusted which offered no slowing or cushioning. Andrew re-entered his home and sat at the reclaimed wood, farmhouse table in the kitchen. With a sip of coffee he was relaxed and ready to examine the contents of the envelope. Inside, there was one paper, a hand-written letter, and a notecard with a time, date and place. He prepared himself for its words as it lay waiting before him.

[Past Lives- Langehorne Slim]

Dear Andrew,
This is Patty. To be honest, I would understand if this is as far as you read, but I hope that you choose to continue. In my ten years here at Northern Pines, I've had plenty of time to reflect on who I am and what I have chosen to do with my life.
The woman writing this is not the woman you once knew. The majority of my life I was a woman with no moral compass. A woman with issues far more disturbing and deplorable than I could have understood or dealt with alone. I was not well, I was not sane. I'd like to believe I am now, but they continue to keep me here. They must be worried that I may stop my medications if I were on my own. I hate thinking that the prescriptions are what have changed me, I'd rather believe I was the catalyst, either way I'm still on them.
Anyway, here, I have been able to face the hard truth that I did these things, these awful things. I have to own my misdeeds, no matter how much I would like to believe, or how much I once believed I was not to blame. While here, I have met wonderful people, who reminded me that there

is always time to make a change. And, that you don't have to be what you once were, you choose who you want to be, but you always have to live with and embrace your past. However, one thing that neither the medication, nor AA, nor my psychologists have been able to change is my hard-headedness. I struggle to make amends, I struggle with the words 'I'm sorry', I struggle with self-deprecation, I struggle. And, I worry that I will die still carrying all the burden created by the old Patty.

And, this, this impossible hurdle has destroyed my relationship with my daughter. She won't return my letters, and I fear it has been too long to mend. And, it has decimated many other people that have passed through my life. I have attempted to make amends with those that I have injured; some listen, some ignore me, but I have tried. The only one I have been unable to garner enough courage to reach out to is you.

You, you and your family have every right to hate me for the rest of your lives. What I did to you, not just the culminating moment but all those that led to it, was reprehensible, abhorred. I am afraid to leave this earth without apologizing, although it might not amount to much to you. I am afraid, for the first time in my life, I am truly afraid, and you hold the key. With all the damage I have caused, with all those in my wake, it is you, you. You are the key to my salvation. It is my hope that one day you will find it in your heart to absolve me of my wrong-doings, for I believe that is the only way I can rest peacefully. Andrew, I am truly sorry for the harmful words, the impossible situations I placed you in. For forcing you to compromise your principles, for

shooting you. I am sorry.
I would be eternally grateful if you were to attend my
funeral, you are the only one I have invited. It is my
dying wish to have your forgiveness, but it is only yours
to give, and I would certainly understand if you decided
otherwise.

Patty Drury

He put the letter back down and sipped the coffee, looking to the ceiling fan for answers. The fly, that also claimed the ceiling fan as his own, peered down, waiting for the moment to torment his 'ol companion, then suddenly and inexplicably flew out the kitchen window. The house was busy, it was Friday in the summer, which meant an early day for his wife and a house full of boys. From the kitchen table he could see Christopher stacking logs for a bonfire and Parker setting up the chairs. His youngest son was digging through the pantry for marshmallows and graham crackers. Life was normal, it was normal and pleasant for eight years. And, for the past five years he hadn't even thought about Patty, except for the occasional glance at the scars on his chest when he exited the shower. Even then, it was fleeting, but now, now it was front and center, screaming in his face just like she used to. He was dumbfounded, saddened and a bit irritated, an odd combination of feelings which mirrored the most odd circumstances. He spent the hours before sunset debating whether or not to tell the family. *Is this legit? Is she really repentant, or is this some sick long-con? —-How can I think that way? Poor lady.* His hand and head began coursing over the scars on his chest and shoulder as he recalled the day. *Give her the benefit. Everyone deserves a chance for redemption...right?*

The low mid-day sun scorched the back of his neck, as it arced over the cloudless skies. His shadow vanished, joining the dark depths of the pit at his feet. A howling wind forced it's way through the thick maple and willow trees which surrounded the burial site. The dusty, bedraggled groundskeeper stood under a low hanging branch in waiting, the shovel propping up his sun-drenched body. This area of the cemetery had yet to be filled, only her plot was labeled. Her original plot was adjoined with Harvey's, but Peter somehow finagled either the legal system or her will to eliminate the possibility of that happening. She was now alone in Brainerd; in a standard casket, with a standard grave marker. There was really no one to blame but herself for the less than ceremonious good-bye.

"Well, Patty." He said to the unadorned casket before him. "I'm not exactly sure what I'm doing here. Part of me just thinks I should let you rot in oblivion. There's also another small part of me that wants to spit on this casket right now." He kicked the mound of loose dirt into the hole below. "But, my wife is right, I'd be remiss to believe that none of what transpired rested on my shoulders. And, to carry this with me the rest of my life is too much of a burden, so I'll submit and give you what you want. You may not deserve it, but I'm in no position to judge that. I only hope your words were genuine and that you finally owned your share in all this. I know I have, but like you I was too hard-headed to reach out, to bury the hatchet. I just shirked the responsibility and avoided you and my whole past life at Drury." He drew his gaze up toward the sky, his eyes flooded with unrestricted sunlight. "I've come to the realization that most people will do what they feel is necessary, even if it's not necessarily right. And, I just need to let them go. I can only control what's in my hands." His eyelids closed, as the negative images swirled around, he brought himself to the words she wanted. "I forgive you Patty. I hope your soul is safe in the loving arms of your Muffin Man."

[No Rain- Blind Melon]

An old, red, rusty truck sat idling at the entrance. Wispy fumes, plumed and rose up, diffusing into the blue sky, while the heavy twang of old country music poured out the windows. Pinning a cigarette between his wrinkled and weathered fingers, the old man tapped the beat on the steering wheel while he waited.

"So?"

"Yep."

"Proud of ya kid."

Introspective and Philosiphical Questions

1. What happened to the shotgun?
2. Who scratched those words into the car?
3. What does the fly represent in this story?
4. How do certain pay-structures and performance evaluation criteria within companies affect managerial behavior?
5. Who is most to blame for the final outcome? Andrew? Patty? Peter? The company? Why?
6. List Patty's specific behaviors: How many were unethical, immoral or illegal. Can acts be unethical but still legal? Can acts be illegal but still moral?
7. Does being medicated for an mental illness mean you are incapable of 'fixing' yourself? If, yes, what does this say about the human condition?
8. How would you diagnose Andrew? Patty? (dark triad?)
9. Was Patty a psychopath? Or just mean?
10. How would the story end if Patty didn't run to face Andrew?
11. Why did the employees at the bakery allow this behavior to go on for so long?
12. What does Andrew mean when he tells Patty, "I know you. I know you all too well."?

About the Author

The author hangs his hat in Buffalo, Minnesota: the rural oasis. Here, he resides with his lovely wife and three energetic boys. Andrew Gentry Madsen graduated magna cum laude with a BS in Business Administration from Metropolitan State University, previously he studied Anthropology at the University of Minnesota- Duluth. He has dabbled in writing for the majority of his life: professional and academic, poetry and fiction. Art, history, music and philosophy have had much influence on his published works. The masterful stories of 'The Stranger' and 'The Picture of Dorian Gray' have had the most impact on his life and personal philosophy. Andrew has more than a decade of experience in the food industry, where he has held roles such as supervisor, manager and corporate trainer. He enjoys open waters, sprawling acres, high mountains, blue skies, bonfires, quiet corners and family time.

If you have any questions or comments regarding the author or this work, feel free to contact the author directly. The author appreciates and prefers the quality and richness of traditional person contact, when compared to social media channels.

andrew.madsen1001@gmail.com
Ph. 651-276-1494

Did you enjoy this book? Then yell it from the mountain tops, or a more reasonable request, tell a friend and write a review on Amazon, Barnes and Noble, or Goodreads.

Also by A. Gentry Madsen

All author profits from the book below are donated to ACA (Adult Children of Alcoholics) and the Minnesota Literacy Council.

Down to Allegory Cove
ISBN978-1329746305
A quarter century's worth of poetry. This collection has something for everyone. It runs the gamut from historical philosophy to modern thought, from doldrums and depression to ecstasy and enthusiasm, from self-exploration to biographical, from concrete science to the inexplicability of human thought and feeling. This condensed collection will force you to think and reexamine yourself and the world around you. Prepare for a journey through the senses. Enjoy.

Made in the USA
Lexington, KY
30 June 2018